A Candlelight Ecstasy Romance®

"LET GO OF ME," CYD MANAGED TO SAY AS SHE WRIGGLED BENEATH HIS STRONG BODY.

"Not until you promise that you won't try to turn me in," Dave told her. He drew in a sharp breath as she squirmed against him. "Will you please lie still?" he said in a raw voice, thinking it was one rotten time to become aware that Cyd was a very desirable woman.

"Not till you let me go. I'm going to scream my bloody head off," Cyd threatened, and then did just that.

Dave interrupted her shriek by covering her mouth with his and kissing her firmly. "Are you going to scream any more?" he demanded when their lips finally separated. "Or am I going to have to kiss you again?"

Be sure to read this month's
CANDLELIGHT ECSTASY CLASSIC ROMANCES . . .

THE TAWNY GOLD MAN, *Amii Lorin*
GENTLE PIRATE, *Jayne Castle*

CANDLELIGHT ECSTASY ROMANCES®

442 FEVER PITCH,
Pamela Toth

443 ONE LOVE FOREVER,
Christine King

444 WHEN LIGHTNING
STRIKES,
Lori Copeland

445 WITH A LITTLE LOVE,
Natalie Stone

446 MORNING GLORY,
Donna Kimel Vitek

447 TAKE-CHARGE LADY,
Alison Tyler

448 ISLAND OF ILLUSIONS,
Jackie Black

449 THE PASSIONATE
SOLUTION,
Jean Hager

FLIGHT OF FANCY

Jane Atkin

A CANDLELIGHT ECSTASY ROMANCE®

Published by
Dell Publishing Co., Inc.
1 Dag Hammarskjold Plaza
New York, New York 10017

Dell ® TM 681510, Dell Publishing Co., Inc.

Candlelight Ecstasy Romance®, 1,203,540, is a registered trademark of Dell Publishing Co., Inc., New York, New York.

ISBN: 0-440-12649-5

Printed in the United States of America

August 1986

10 9 8 7 6 5 4 3 2 1

WFH

With all my love to Steven, Andrew, and Beth.

To Our Readers:

We have been delighted with your enthusiastic response to Candlelight Ecstasy Romances®, and we thank you for the interest you have shown in this exciting series.

In the upcoming months we will continue to present the distinctive sensuous love stories you have come to expect only from Ecstasy. We look forward to bringing you many more books from your favorite authors and also the very finest work from new authors of contemporary romantic fiction.

As always, we are striving to present the unique, absorbing love stories that you enjoy most—books that are more than ordinary romance. Your suggestions and comments are always welcome. Please write to us at the address below.

Sincerely,

The Editors
Candlelight Romances
1 Dag Hammarskjold Plaza
New York, New York 10017

FLIGHT OF FANCY

CHAPTER ONE

"My boss told me to tell you that he had quite a bit of trouble finding these three-quarter-inch square-tipped nailheads," said Eddie Scanlon while taking inventory.

Cydney Knight placed her right hand on her slim hip, transferring her weight. She slanted her head, assumed a pose, and waited out the kid's inspection. Eddie's eyes were on her faded denim vest jacket and oversized beige cotton shirt. Somewhere along the line the kid must have decided he was the "bad boy" type. He was playing the role to the hilt.

"He had to call four different factories," Eddie continued while he inspected Cyd's well-fitted jeans covering the stretch of her long shapely legs. His gaze made it all the way down to the flat lilac sandals tied at her ankles.

"Well, now you have them. How about going behind the counter and writing me up a sales slip so that I can get going?" Cyd asked, amused.

Eddie's attention came back up sharply to her face. "I just bet you had a rough day," he drawled before walking behind the counter.

"I bet if I said I did you would suggest that you could make it better?" Cyd squelched a smirk.

"Took the words right out of my mouth." Eddie grinned.

"Before you get too carried away, I want you to know that I do believe in preliminaries," Cyd said challengingly, deciding to be gentle with his ego. "For starters, dinner at a nice intimate restaurant . . . one where they even charge for the water . . . and dancing. . . . Hey, listen, I'm not going to be embarrassed when you're proofed, am I?"

"I could get my brother's driver's license. We look alike. But as far as the restaurant goes . . . I'm kind of broke. I'm saving up to pay my tuition. I'm starting college in the fall."

"Oh, what a shame," Cyd said, debating whether or not to bat her long, dark brown eyelashes. "Here I was looking forward to an evening with a real man." She emphasized the last two words, letting it go at that.

"Yeah . . . well, sometimes you can't get everything you want." Eddie Scanlon hurriedly wrote out the sales slip, thinking it was just as well that it hadn't worked out. He might not have been able to pull it off. She'd probably laugh her head off if she found out he hadn't yet lost his innocence.

"The story of my life," Cyd remarked, pretending disappointment as she paid for the nails. The smile she'd been holding back played on her lips as she walked away from the counter.

Once outside the lumberyard, Cyd checked her watch. She still had a little more than an hour to prepare the special dinner she'd planned for Josh. She was really stretching her budget on this meal. Cyd grinned as she thought, the way to a man's heart might very well be through his stomach. Sometimes, more often

12

lately, she wondered about her relationship with Josh. Deep inside, she knew she'd hoped to feel more. Not that she didn't feel quite a bit, Cyd assured herself. In fact, she had very little to complain about. Their temperaments matched most of the time. They had similar likes and similar dislikes. All in all they had quite a bit going for them. So what if that hyped-up pie-in-the-sky thrill was missing? She'd work on it.

Coming up to her car, a 1972 Ford Maverick, Cyd cursed under her breath. She'd been wedged in between a Caddy and the lumberyard's delivery truck. She was just about to turn around and go into the yard to ask them to move the truck when a man wearing a thin nylon windbreaker with the Griffith Lumberyard logo stepped out through a rear door.

"Could you get going? I'm blocked in," Cyd called out impatiently, getting into her car.

Not even bothering to look her way, the delivery man jumped into the back of the truck and started going over the contents stacked there against a list he was holding. Still not turning, the man gave her a backward wave of his hand, fingers spread. Cyd took the gesture to mean five minutes.

This was the fifth delivery of the day. David Bradley hoped it would be the last. He wasn't used to manual labor. The only wood he'd ever pushed around had an eraser on one end. Flexing his arms, Dave tried to ease the knots in his muscles as he checked to make sure he had loaded the truck exactly to the delivery list.

Cyd gave her watch another look. It had to be more than five minutes. Not feeling particularly patient, she tapped her horn.

Deliberately oblivious to the honking, Dave continued to work through the list.

Cyd punched the horn again, this time pressing down for one steady blast.

Angry now, Dave turned, squatted down, ready to chew her head off about being patient, but the words got stuck in his throat, along with his breath. He wouldn't have called her beautiful, only because he didn't particularly care for red heads, though her hair was more a deep auburn than red. Besides that he preferred very long hair on women. Hers just about reached her shoulders. But then again he had to concede that red hair seemed just right for her. And on second thought, he decided, she was smart not to wear her hair too long. It might have detracted from the impact of her very large, darkly fringed, cinnamon-brown eyes. But even more than her dramatic eyes there was something very special about her that made her stand out, yet he couldn't put his finger on it. It came to him finally that the real turn-on, for him anyway, was a sense that she was perfectly in tune to her sexuality and totally comfortable about it. From the flush of pleasure on her high cheekbones, he was certain she was enjoying his assessment.

Some days, Cyd thought, you walk around feeling almost invisible, and then back-to-back you get showered with appreciation. Go figure it?

"Two more minutes," Dave called out before turning back to his task. Beginning to feel uncomfortably warm now that it was no longer raining, Dave slipped off his thin windbreaker.

For a second Cyd wondered if he was staging a show for her, directing her to watch the performance of his muscles, clearly visible through his white T-shirt. If it

14

was intentional, he had succeeded. He had her full attention. She couldn't stop looking at his hard, lean body as he restacked some wood. Turning, Dave caught her watching him intently. He smiled. Crazy, but all of a sudden Cyd had the strangest feeling of déjà vu. She could swear they had met before today.

Finished going over the list, Dave jumped down from the rear of the truck and walked over to Cyd's car. He placed one hand on the Naugahyde roof, which was constantly peeling and which she continually repaired with an assortment of glues. "Sorry I held you up," he apologized.

"That's okay," Cyd answered, thinking that her voice missed sounding normal.

Dave took his hand off the roof of the car, a swatch of discolored beige Naugahyde stuck to his fingers. "Here" —he grinned—"I guess you want this." Pulling the piece of roofing from his fingers, he handed it to her.

She laughed. "Next time I glue the top I think I should sleep on it to make sure it sticks." Cyd took the tear of the car's roofing and flung it nonchalantly onto the backseat. She had that feeling again. The feeling that she knew this guy from somewhere. The simplest explanation was that she'd noticed him sometime before right here at the lumberyard. Since she'd started her unique furniture venture she'd made many a visit to Griffith's. "Have you been working here for long?" Cyd asked.

"No, but I'm glad it doesn't show. This is only my second day."

"You don't sound like you come from New York and definitely not from Brooklyn."

"I've been here for only three days. I was born in

15

Oregon, but I've spent most of my life in California."
Dave smiled and thought of asking for a date, then he
reminded himself he had no time for romance. He already had enough on his hands.

"This is not a line," Cyd clarified. "But I have this
really strong feeling we've met before."

"If we had met before, I would have remembered,"
Dave said, feeling his body tense. Then he shrugged
aside his unease. It was ridiculous to go around feeling
jumpy all the time.

"That's what makes it so strange," Cyd said, smiling.
"I would have thought I'd have remembered too." One
doesn't easily forget a man with those blue eyes and that
fantastic head of thick, dark blond hair. Odd, Cyd had
the impression that he didn't know the effect his ex-
traordinary good looks had on women.

"I'm Dave Bradley." He extended his hand through
the window of her car. He liked the way she just came
right out and said what she thought.

"Cydney Knight . . . that's with a *C.*" She pumped
his hand and it turned on a current of electricity. These
things don't happen—but nevertheless a surge of heat
spiraled throughout her body, then rose to her cheeks.
Subdued, probably for the first time in her life, Cyd met
Dave's eyes reluctantly. She was concerned that he
would read her reaction, yet she wanted to know if he
felt it too.

You read about sparks, Dave thought. The ones arc-
ing between them were strong enough to light the Los
Angeles freeway. He found himself once again trying to
work up the courage to ask her out. It was a long time
since he'd played the dating game. "Sorry again,
Cydney with a *C,* for the holdup. It was real nice meet-

ing you." He smiled once more and then hurried off for the cab of the truck. Under the circumstances it would be smarter to leave well enough alone. It was too risky to get involved.

Cyd watched Dave's agile movement as he hoisted himself up into the driver's seat. She couldn't get over his astonishingly good looks and the feeling that she had definitely seen him before. But where? . . . And then it hit her like a ton of bricks. In shock, Cyd knew exactly why he looked so familiar. She'd paused to stare in appreciation at his picture on a wanted poster after she'd finished licking twenty stamps to send out a batch of overdue bills yesterday at the post office. It had struck her at the time that it was a shame that a guy who looked so handsome was also a criminal. She couldn't remember if she'd bothered to note the name of the man on the poster, but there was no doubt in her mind that Dave Bradley was also the guy in the picture. And if she remembered correctly—and she was sure she did—there was a reward of $10,000 for information leading to his arrest. The dollar sign had caught her attention even before she'd looked at his face. The only thing she couldn't remember noticing was the crime he'd committed. Great! For all she knew she could have been chatting away with a murderer.

Where the hell were the cops when you needed them? "Hey, Dave, hold it," Cyd screamed, jumping out of her car to run into the middle of the road. She dashed back up on the curb after being nearly run over. At the top of her lungs, her hands cupped around her mouth, she hollered, "Wait up, Dave," without any idea of what she'd do if he did. As it turned out, she needn't have worried. She wasn't able to get Dave's attention. But she was getting noticed by a number of passersby. "He forgot to take his umbrella," Cyd ad-libbed to a couple of elderly ladies shaking their heads distastefully at her as she charged back for her car.

Shifting into gear, Cyd floored the gas pedal, managing in the heavy traffic to keep the Griffith lumber truck in sight. Her mind was working a mile a minute—not that she was coming up with any definite plan. Impulsive as usual, Cyd decided she'd figure out what to do once she caught up to him.

Dave didn't need to check the street map he carried. He'd made this run yesterday. He held the wheel as lightly as possible as he swung the truck. His blistered hands were hurting. But for the first time since his problems began, his mind was swapping fear for some pleasanter thoughts. Those thoughts all centered around Cydney Knight. He even liked the ring of her name, and so he said it aloud a few times while he let his very active imagination take over.

What pure dumb luck, Cyd was thinking, already counting the reward money. . . . She'd really be able to get her furniture venture off the ground floor. No more part-time jobs. If she budgeted tightly, she could make the money stretch for at least three months, maybe four, even with sharing half of her windfall with Josh. It would be fabulous if Josh could devote his full time to sculpturing . . . no more staggering home at 3 A.M. after waiting on tables all night. And she could stop worrying that he seemed to be a bit distant lately. Cyd was sure all Josh needed was some regular hours of sleep.

Humming "Happy Days Are Here Again," Cyd kept Dave's truck in sight.

Then as all good things do . . . Cyd's 1972 Maverick belched and came to a full stop, stalling traffic. She remembered then that she was going to fill the tank after she picked up the nails at Griffith's. She'd driven to work on empty in the morning, knowing the tank still held four gallons.

Banging her hands on the steering wheel, Cyd listened to a bevy of inarticulate complaints mingle with the sound of honking horns.

Storming out of her car, Cyd held up her hands in aggravation. "I'm out of gas. . . . What do you want me to do?" she yelled.

"Yah screwball . . . when did you fill up? I bet you didn't even check the tank." The pouchy-faced middle-aged guy owning the voice got out of a spanking-new Oldsmobile directly in back of Cyd's car. His companion, another male Weight Watchers reject, pushed open the passenger door. "There should be a law about keeping these junk boxes off the road . . . along with dames," came the latter's input.

Cyd decided there was nothing like a little balance to set the ego back in line. "Shall I go for coffee and we can debate the merits of female drivers versus males, or would you like to help me out?" She took a stance with her hands on her hips.

"Smart aleck! What would you like us to do?" the driver of the Oldsmobile asked angrily.

"Let's do something." The request came from farther up the line of halted cars.

"How about someone giving me a push to the curb?" Cyd suggested. After a few minutes of hassling over who would actually do the pushing, she got her request.

Her Maverick was pushed to the curb right in line with a fire hydrant.

"Thanks a lot," Cyd grumbled between clenched teeth as her rescuers took off. She'd just been neatly set up for a ticket.

Calming down, Cyd realized that was the least of her problems. She had long since lost sight of Dave Bradley. Options? . . . She could notify Art Griffith, the owner of the lumberyard, that he had a "wanted man" in his employ. Only the chances were he'd want a split of the reward money. He might even feel he was entitled to the whole thing. Cyd quickly cast that idea aside. She could call the police directly and report Dave Bradley's whereabouts. But what if they bungled the capture? She could see it now. A bunch of police cars converging on the lumberyard, sirens screeching, giving Dave Bradley advance warning. Cyd wasn't going to risk her money that way, and that took care of all the possibilities she could come up with off the top of her head—not that she considered herself stumped—not by a long shot. There had to be one more idea—the perfect one—rattling around in her brain. She would just have to think a little bit harder, which lead her to consider the prospect of attempting to capture Dave Bradley on her own. . . . That was a crazy idea and she knew it. But then again, she needn't be completely on her own. There was Josh waiting in her apartment. She'd offered him the use of her place in the afternoon to do his sculpting. The furnished back-alley flat he rented was too small and cluttered for him to spread out.

Cyd headed for the pay phone on the corner and called home. Josh answered the phone on the fourth ring.

". . . And I've got a fabulous plan how we can capture him," Cyd told Josh after she'd brought him up to date. The more she thought about it, the more certain she became that together they could pull this off.

"I can hardly wait to hear this," Josh answered brusquely.

"Come on, Josh. Give me a little enthusiasm," Cyd said coaxingly.

"What if the guy's dangerous? He could even be a madman. Besides that, have you ever considered that you might be mistaken and that he might not be the man in the poster? You said the guy gave you his name, but you can't remember if the guy in the poster had the same name."

"Josh, I'm certain he's the man. You know I have this thing for faces. Anyway, he's probably not using his real name. And even if he is dangerous, it's going to be two against one. Plus, we will have the advantage of a surprise attack," Cyd assured him.

"Yeah"—Josh sighed—"right." Two months ago she'd set up an easel on Bleecker Street in Greenwich Village, certain she had a flair for drawing caricatures because she had a great eye for faces. She hadn't sold one of her pictures. "What's your plan?" Josh asked, thinking that if his own plan worked out he might not be around to deal with Cyd's.

"I'm going to head back to the lumberyard and place an order. I'll insist that it has to be delivered immediately or no sale. Then I'll grab a cab and get back to the apartment. Between us, I'm sure we can overpower him." Now that her mind was made up, she had no intention of giving up the idea.

"Why are you going to take a cab? What happened to

your car?" Josh was pacing back and forth in the living room in front of a casement window that was on the same level as the street.

"It's a long story. I'll explain later. Promise me that you won't go to work tonight. I don't know how long this will take. Call in sick or something."

"Right," Josh answered, quickly hanging up. He'd spotted Gloria Crane's Mercedes turning the corner.

When you don't want to see a cop here they are doing their duty. "One of New York's finest" was in the process of writing Cyd up a ticket for parking in front of a fire hydrant when she got back to her car.

"This car belong to you?" the officer asked.

"Yes," Cyd answered.

"If you move it right now, it's only going to cost you a fifty-dollar ticket."

"I'm out of gas," Cyd explained.

"Then I'm going to have to call the tow truck," the officer responded indifferently.

"How much is it going to cost me to claim it?"

"A hundred bucks," was the answer. With an appraising eye, the officer considered the probability that the car wasn't worth that much.

Exasperated, Cyd sighed. "Did you ever have one of those days when you get teased into thinking everything is going to go right and then nothing does?"

The officer cracked a smile. "I know what you mean," he said sympathetically, but that didn't deter him from reaching into his car for the radio to call for a tow truck.

Cyd left him making arrangements to pick up her car and walked back to the corner, keeping her eye out for a cab. There was one bright light. It was Saturday and she had her pay in the worn gray backpack she had slung over her shoulder. This could have happened yesterday when she was flat broke and wouldn't have had the money to take a cab.

Griffith's was a half hour away from closing, and just about empty when Cyd returned to the yard. Eddie Scanlon, the young boy who had waited on her earlier, had already left for the day. Mr. Griffith himself was totaling out the registers.

"Hi, Cyd. Weren't you here earlier?" Art Griffith strove for a one-to-one approach with his customers. He made sure he got to know his regulars by their first names.

"I was." Cyd smiled. "I got home and realized I was out of oak boards. I really need six pieces in a hurry. Art, can you do me a big favor and have it delivered this evening?"

"The truck should be back in about fifteen minutes, but it was the last run for today."

"Here I have this burst of energy and nothing to work with. Isn't that always the way?" Cyd turned on her most endearing little-girl look.

"I can't promise you," Art said, responding to her expression. "But I'll tell you what. . . . I'll talk to my delivery man when he gets back."

"You can tell him that I'll tip him generously if he'll make this one last delivery. Now why don't you write up my order while I pick out the pieces I'd like?" Cyd traded her little-girl look for her most charming smile.

Art came around the counter, order pad in hand, and escorted Cyd to the piles of oak wood.

Dave's heart leapt as he spotted Cydney talking to his boss. He'd just pushed aside the urge to check and see if her phone number was listed, and here she was looking even more sensational now that he had a full view of her out of the confines of her car.

"Dave . . ." Art noticed him first and called him over. "This is one of my very best customers. She just realized she's out of oak boards and she needs six boards in a hurry. Now I know you just finished up, but you would be doing me a big favor if you'd just make one more trip."

"Sure." Dave agreed quickly. "Only instead of bringing the truck back tonight, how about I bring it back on Monday?" He felt terrific. All his aches and pains had miraculously disappeared. Cydney Knight was really something. She saw what she wanted and she didn't let any grass grow under her feet. Later he'd tell her she could have come right out and just asked instead of setting up an excuse to get him to her apartment.

"Well, I guess that would be okay," Art answered, reluctant to let a new employee keep the truck, but realizing that under the circumstances he couldn't refuse. He handed Dave the order slip with Cyd's address.

"See you in about twenty minutes," Cyd told Dave, not looking at him directly. "And thanks, Art," Cyd added before walking away. So far, so good, thought Cyd. Now all she had to do was find a cab, get back to the apartment, and make sure Josh was standing ready.

Dave saw Cyd as he turned the first block away from the lumberyard. She was trying to whistle down an off-duty cab. "What happened to your car?" he called out.

"I had some problems before and had to have it towed away," Cyd answered, irritated. What rotten luck! The way it looked now Dave Bradley was going to get to her apartment, unload the wood, and take off

24

before she even found a cab. Cyd was certain Josh wouldn't try to capture him without her egging him on.

With a grin, Dave said, "Seems to me we're both heading in the same direction. Hop in."

Cyd took a second to think it over. Praying he wasn't wanted for murder, she walked around the front of the truck and got in. No risk—no reward.

"What are you planning to do with the wood?" Dave asked idly as he drove. Having a woman, one he hardly even knew, come right out and proposition him was something that had never happened to him before.

"I design and make furniture," Cyd responded tightly. She was staring straight ahead. Taut with tension, her body was pressed close to the door, keeping as much room between them as possible.

Perplexed by her unexpected attitude, Dave eyed her profile for the merest second. "I've never met a lady who made furniture before. Have you been doing it for long?" he asked, doing his part to get a conversation going. He had no objection to some casual sex, but he thought it would be nice if they got to know each other a little before they jumped into bed.

"Not long," Cyd replied. "You make a right at the next light, go straight for two blocks, and then you make a left." She wished he would just stop talking to her.

"Cydney?" Dave paused. He wanted to tell her how sexy he thought she was and that he really liked the idea that she'd taken the initiative and made the first approach. "Would you like to stop for something to eat first?" he asked instead of saying what he had on his mind.

Cyd flashed a sharp look at him. "I don't want to

25

have anything to eat," she said, exasperated. "Can't you drive any faster?" With the way her luck had been going lately, Josh could be walking out the door on his way to work this very minute.

Hell . . . if she was going to rush him like this he might not be able to perform. Dave decided to keep his mouth shut for a while and think this through. The converted brownstone she lived in came up before he'd thought any of it out.

"It's the basement apartment," Cyd said, jumping out of the truck as soon as it came to a halt. The only reason she took note of the Mercedes parked against the curb with a heavily made-up brunette at the wheel was because those kinds of bucks were out of place in this end of the Flatbush section of Brooklyn, New York.

Cyd flung open the door to her apartment and found Josh shoving all his sculpting material into a suitcase. Josh looked at her guiltily for a few seconds before saying, "I've left you a note. I think we should just cool it for a while." Josh averted his eyes and closed his suitcase.

"What the hell do you mean . . . you think we should cool it for a while?" Cyd took a quick look around. All the projects he'd been working on were gone.

"Stay calm, Cyd," Josh said, starting to circle around her. "I explained it all in the note."

Seething, Cyd glared at him as she deliberately blocked his way. "I don't want to read any notes. I want you to say what you have to say to me to my face."

Dave banged on the door. He was holding the first of the six planks of oak she'd ordered under one arm. "Come in," Cyd screamed at him.

Dave entered and looked from Cyd to Josh. He certainly hadn't expected to find a man in her apartment, though this one seemed to be on the way out. Maybe she'd gotten wind that her boyfriend was leaving and she'd gone out shopping for a replacement.

"Any place special you want me to stack this?" Dave asked. Not receiving any answer, he dropped the oak boards to the floor.

"I can't keep up this pace any longer. I've got to start sleeping at night," Josh answered Cyd as Dave headed for the door.

So that was the reason Cydney Knight had moved in on him so fast, Dave concluded on his way out. She was one of those women who couldn't be deprived of sex even for one night.

"What do you want to do, Cyd, fight? You said yourself you weren't sure if this was going to work out," Josh went on after Dave left to finish unloading the truck.

"Nice of you to make up both our minds," Cyd said hotly. "I suppose you've got someone else on the line."

Josh's voice rose above Cyd's. "What difference does that make?"

"It makes a big difference," Cyd said, not exactly sure what the difference was except that her pride was hurt. "Wait a minute . . ." She raced across the room and halted at the casement window. "It's that overdressed, overstuffed brunette in the Mercedes, isn't it?"

Not bothering to knock, Dave walked back into the apartment struggling to carry three pieces of wood at a time. The sooner he finished up, the sooner he could get out of here. He was sure he didn't have the staying power—or the energy—to fill her demands.

"You're right. It's the brunette in the Mercedes," Josh was saying. "Gloria has been coming here every day for the past week while you've been at work and posing for me."

"I knew it . . . I just knew it," Cyd said caustically, voicing what she'd already surmised. "The top half of that nude you said you were doing of me . . . isn't me."

Dave's admiration went to the boyfriend. The guy must have some stamina. Laying down the wood quickly, Dave went out to get the last of it. He could hear the two of them tearing into each other all the way down the hall.

Josh was opening the door to step out when Dave got back with the balance of the order. Cyd elbowed Dave aside to call after Josh, "What about my plan? You agreed to help me."

"It's your plan," Josh said over his shoulder. "Thanks for the offer, but I don't need half of ten thousand measly bucks now."

Cyd threw her backpack at him. It hit Josh in the head. He picked it up and threw it back at her. Cyd ducked. It landed at her feet inside the apartment.

Dave coughed in an attempt to gain Cyd's attention. "That's all of it," he said, anxious to get going. "You can straighten the bill with Mr. Griffith."

Cyd closed the door and turned to give Dave a long, studied look while she tried to suppress the thought of trying to capture him alone. She guessed Bradley to be just about six feet tall, which gave him a good six inches on her. Then again she had taken twelve karate lessons, and her instructor had told her she was making fine progress before she decided to quit. That had to count

28

for something. Plus, she still had the advantage of surprise. She'd need control and steel nerves. She'd also have to make her move soon. He looked like he was getting very antsy to get on his way.

"I'll pay for the wood now," Cyd said, honey melting in her mouth. Dave took the bill out of his pocket as he watched her walk over to the oak boards. He figured she was going to look the wood over before she gave him any money. She bent down, picked up a piece, and then, waving the board in the air, she screamed and lunged for him.

CHAPTER TWO

Dave sidestepped just in time. "What the hell is the matter with you?" he yelled, struggling to get the slab of wood out of her hands.

Not answering, Cyd fought to hold on. Her karate lessons didn't seem to help too much, and after a few minutes of struggle he knocked the wood out of her hands. Without losing any momentum, Cyd jumped him, pushing Dave to the floor. He rolled her over, pinning her beneath him. Still she managed to get in one good punch before he pressed her hands down flat above her head.

He could still feel the hot sting on his jaw where her fist had landed. More bewildered than angered, Dave pulled in a shaken breath. "What is it with you? Are you trying to rape me?"

"Rape you?" Those great big cinnamon-brown eyes of hers flashed with astonishment. "I'm trying to make a citizen's arrest," she spat out, doing her best to shift out from under the weight of his body.

Thrown off balance, Dave loosened his hold on her hands. Cyd took immediate advantage, pulling completely free to push at his chest. Maneuvering her legs, Cyd worked a wrestler's hold and traded places with him. Breathing heavily, he flipped her back around. "I'm not a criminal," Dave rasped, lying over her again.

"Don't play innocent with me. I saw your picture on a wanted poster in the post office," Cyd retorted. She listened to the pounding of her heart while she tried to anticipate his next move. At the very least, he was probably going to knock her senseless.

He watched her face carefully. "You're crazy. . . . You've made a mistake," he said.

"I'm crazy? Fine . . . Let's go down to the post office and we'll see who's crazy," she taunted, totally forgetting her compromising position.

He'd never considered the possibility that his picture would make the walls of the post offices all the way here on the East Coast, in the borough of Brooklyn, no less. "There are hundreds of people who look alike." He gave her the best he could come up with as an explanation.

She didn't buy it. "If I were you and someone told me that there was a criminal who looked enough like me to be my double, I'd want to check it out."

"I guess that's where we differ. I'm not the least bit interested."

"Well, maybe the police will be interested in checking the comparison when I report where you're working." She regretted the statement as soon as she had made it. She'd just given him every reason to shut her up—permanently. The only hope she could come up with for herself was that she wasn't able to feel a gun in his pockets or under his belt. The only bulge she could feel clearly enough was the one part of his anatomy she forced herself to ignore.

"I can't have you messing up my one chance." He groaned, turned his head, and then was quiet.

"Then I am right," Cyd said spontaneously.

Dave didn't answer immediately. "I'm being framed," he said after the pause. He was still trying to think up some way to reason with her.

Isn't that what they all say? "What are you being framed for?" Cyd asked, deciding her best move was to pretend she believed whatever lie he handed her. It didn't look like she was going to be able to capture him, not at the moment anyway.

Confused, Dave looked into her eyes—eyes that consistently wowed him. "I thought you said you saw my picture on a wanted poster?"

Cyd turned her head and answered into his shoulder, "I did. I just can't remember your crime."

"You mean you took a chance trying to capture me without knowing what I was supposed to have done? What if I was a murderer?" Dave decided she was truly one of a kind.

"Are you?" She stared at him without blinking. Somewhere she remembered it was important not to look afraid. But that might have been a protection against a charging dog, not a criminal.

"I'm not a murderer. I'm being framed for a land-development scheme. They might be calling it mail fraud. I'm not sure." His voice had a knot in it.

Cyd sighed and didn't care if he heard it. "I will say that I'm glad that you're not a murderer. Now why don't you let me get up and then you can tell me the whole story?"

"If I let you up, you're probably going to try and hit me over the head again."

He had her number. "If you're not going to let me get up, do you think that you could maybe ease off a little?" she requested angrily. "I can hardly breathe."

It didn't seem to Dave that she was having any trouble breathing. Nor did it feel that way. Her firm breasts were moving steadily against his chest, keeping him very aware of her softness. She really had a fabulous body, all sleek and slender. "Do you always go around trying to capture criminals?" he asked.

"You're my first." Her brown eyes continued to flash at him defiantly.

"What's in this for you?" He felt the need to understand her motivation.

"There's a reward on your head. Ten thousand dollars to be exact, Mr. Bradley, or whatever your name is."

"My name is David Bradley," he said dryly. As if things weren't bad enough. Now he had a reward on his head. He could probably look forward to having every Tom, Dick, and Harry chase him down for the money.

"Do you mean to tell me you're using your real name? It's a wonder someone didn't catch onto you sooner." Either this guy was dumb or he didn't watch TV.

"Everyone's got smart answers when it isn't their problem. Excuse me for not realizing that my fame had spread to the East Coast," Dave said heatedly, responding to the censure in Cyd's tone. He could feel himself becoming unglued, and he'd always prided himself on being able to keep his cool no matter what the circumstances.

"If you're hiding out, the first thing you should have thought of was to change your name, and, second, you

33

should have done something to change your appearance. Don't you know that with your looks you could be picked out easily, even in a crowd?"

"Well, I'm terribly sorry." Dave really exploded, which was totally out of character for him. "This is the first time I've ever been wanted by the law. All I've been thinking about is trying to catch up to the people who framed me. I'm sure the two of them are in New York."

"Who framed you?" Cyd asked, not that she was swallowing the idea for one minute.

"My ex-wife and her new husband, who also happened to be my accountant."

Give me a break, she thought. "That sounds cozy."

"It's very cozy," Dave concurred, not realizing that she was being derisive. "Joe Thomas was not just my accountant. He was also my best friend."

"You mean to tell me that your wife left you for your best friend? I thought I had problems," she said sarcastically.

"Actually, after I thought it over I decided it was a blessing in disguise." He wished he knew how to defuse her.

What kind of guy was so complacent about losing his wife to his best friend? Her guess was that he was making the whole story up.

"Don't get me wrong," Dave was going on. "Hollis can really be terrific provided you're not married to her."

"I'd love to hear all about Hollis," Cyd said sweetly. "How about—"

"I'm not letting you get up if that's what you're angling for," Dave said cutting her off.

34

"Fine," Cyd snarled, wriggling beneath him in an attempt to free herself.

Dave drew in a sharp breath as she squirmed against his body. It was a hell of a moment for him to be aware that she was every inch a very desirable woman. "Will you please lie still?" he said in a raw voice.

"I'm going to scream my bloody head off," Cyd threatened, and then she did just that.

Dave interrupted her shriek just as she was really getting warmed up. Cyd bit his bottom lip as his mouth covered hers. He bit her right back, but not quite as hard. "That hurt," Cyd complained.

"I know," Dave confirmed, running his tongue over his lower lip. "Are you going to scream again?"

"No," she said nastily.

"God . . . I can't believe I'm behaving this way. I have never in my life hurt a woman before." He pounded the floor with his hand. Since he still had her hand in his grasp, she took the brunt of his distress.

"Forget it. My hand can't handle any more of your agitation," she said cuttingly while looking into his unforgettable blue eyes. He looked so miserable, she almost regretted the tone of her voice.

"Did I hurt you again?" He looked even more miserable as he rotated her slim hand in his firm grasp and checked for a bruise. "I'm really sorry. Please believe me. Everything is so crazy. Did you ever wake up one morning and find that your whole world had turned upside down?"

"Do you think that you've cornered the market?" Cyd muttered, and then her voice rose. "This has not been one of my favorite days. First, Jensen gives me a talking-to because I let a customer get away without making a purchase. I tried every size nine shoe in the store on her, and she couldn't get her feet into any of them. I told her she was a size ten and not a size nine, and she just upped and walked out. You think Jensen is interested in hearing excuses? He's not. The only thing he's interested in hearing is the ring of the register. Straight from this great part-time job of mine I go to Griffith's and run into you. I realize who you are and I go chasing after you. Guess what happens next? I wind up having my car towed away. And if you think that's not enough . . . to cap it all off I come home and find Josh dumping me for some brunette with big bucks." Her voice cracked on the last. On a conscious level she resisted examining the shortcomings in her relationship with Josh—shortcomings that had recently become quite apparent. She chose instead to concentrate on her feelings of rejection.

"You're really upset about that guy, aren't you?"

"Are you for real? Of course I'm upset. Do you know how many dates I've been on in just this past year? . . . You go out with the need to prove yourself—make sure you're showing your best side—and then when you feel satisfied that you couldn't have come across any better, you realize it wasn't worth the effort. Do you know how hard it is to find someone who you at least have a few things in common with? I've been going with Josh for three months now. I thought it was really working out. . . . It might have worked out with some more time."

"It doesn't sound to me like you're too sure about that."

"What are you, a psychologist too?" Cyd asked, infuriated.

36

"I was just trying to lend a shoulder. . . . Forget it," Dave said, vexed.

"Maybe what Josh and I had wasn't perfect. . . . Maybe it wasn't even all that good. But I'll tell you something. . . . I don't like being dumped." She admitted what was partially bothering her. At twenty-seven she was beginning to worry about ever finding a relationship really worth hanging on to. Either she was breaking one off or they were.

"I know how it feels," Dave commiserated. "Personally, I think Josh should have his eyes checked. I wish I knew what else to say to you to make you feel better."

"Stop crushing me to death and I'll feel a whole lot better," Cyd muttered. She'd be damned if she was going to thank him for his compliment or indicate in any way that she'd been privately pleased by his flattering remark. He was a criminal. And even if he wasn't a criminal, she wasn't about to be suckered into believing any guy's sweet talk ever again.

Dave eased off her, but only slightly. He wasn't going to take any chance that she would do something crazy. "Do you believe that I've been telling you the truth about being framed?" he asked.

"Listen, buddy, you haven't explained very much."

"Would you really like to hear the whole story?"

"Sure, I really want to hear the whole story." What choice did she have? He'd made her a captive audience.

Dave cleared his throat. "I'm still putting all the pieces together myself. I guess it all started with the divorce. You see, the judge awarded Hollis a percentage of my business."

"That doesn't sound fair," Cyd said suspiciously. "If

she divorced you, why should she be entitled to a part of your business?"

"It was her argument that she had supported me for the first year of our marriage, until I got things going. The judge agreed that she should be compensated. I'll tell you the truth, I wasn't that upset about it. Hollis's share didn't give her any voting rights. It worked out better for me that way than having to come up with a cash settlement. I try and throw all my profits back into my business. The thing of it was, I was gullible enough to believe that everything was going to work out among the three of us. I honestly thought that we would all remain friends."

Gullible? If he was telling the truth, he was weird. . . . "I suppose then that they turned the tables on you." She played along.

"I should have suspected that something was up when Hollis insisted that I take a nice long vacation after they came back from their honeymoon. I'll tell you, in the five years that I was married to Hollis I'd never known her to put herself out very much for me, not that she wasn't always there for her friends. Anyway, here she was willing to give up her aerobic classes, her tennis lessons, and her lunches with the girls, all to let me get away for three weeks and take a much needed rest. I'll say this, I was impressed."

"You mean you took off and Hollis and her new husband raked you over the coals."

"Exactly," Dave confirmed. "I first found out that I was wanted by the FBI when I picked up a newspaper on my flight home from Mexico. The paper said that I had supposedly bilked a group of investors out of a small fortune in a phony land-development scheme. It didn't take long for me to put two and two together, especially once I found out that Hollis and Joe had taken off for parts unknown."

"You said you were looking for them. What makes you think they would be here in New York?" His story was so outlandish, she almost believed him.

"Hollis's parents live here. If the two of them are not here, then her parents know where they are. Hollis didn't even go to the bathroom without reporting it first to her mother." Dave shifted his weight a little to get more comfortable.

Cyd tensed. The distinct sensuality of his body moving against hers was provoking some wildly disturbing sensations. "Have you tried to contact her mother?" Cyd asked, giving him a cool, hard look to cover up her distress.

"I've been calling her like clockwork since I arrived in New York. She hangs up as soon as she hears my voice."

"That sounds like it could mean something," Cyd had to admit.

"Not necessarily . . . she never cared for me. Right from the start she decided that I wasn't good enough for her daughter."

"Oh . . . one of those." Cyd caught herself smiling. She quickly rearranged her expression into a frown.

"Do you have a mother who thinks that the guy hasn't been born that's good enough for you?"

"A father. Although he may have revised his opinion of my merits."

"Why is that?" Dave asked with a grin.

"Look, Dave, how about letting me get up now? I'll tell you all about it over a cup of coffee," she said nonchalantly, even though that electrically charged body of his was beginning to ignite a spark that inspired a different kind of panic.

Dave was beginning to feel a tension of a different kind too—one he recognized all too well. "I still don't think I can trust you." He studied her suspiciously, concentrating on the circumstances and not on the composition of her body beneath his while he made a determined effort not to physically give away the wayward direction of his thoughts.

"Well, we can't lie on the floor forever," Cyd reasoned with him. "And you've already proved that you're stronger than me. What can I possibly do?" She had the feeling she was never going to forget the imprint of his body over hers.

"I don't know. I hear your mind clicking away." He was starting to break out in a cold sweat—then in a hot sweat. The hot one was worse.

"You want to know what I'm thinking . . ." Cyd thought real fast. "I'm thinking I'd like to get into something more comfortable. The very first thing I do when I get home from work is get undressed." She lowered her eyelashes seductively and then opened her eyes wide, watching for his reaction. He didn't seem to be going for the bait, so she pulled out all the stops, dished out her sexiest smile, and toned her voice down to a bare murmur. "How about a glass of wine instead of the coffee? We could put on some music, relax, and you can tell me all about yourself. Come on, Dave, let me up."

"Let me think about it," Dave answered, wondering what clothes she thought of as "more comfortable."

"Could you hurry up?" Cyd said sweetly.

For a long moment all he thought about was the fresh

smell of her hair, the feel of her body. "All right. I'll let you get up. But just remember that I am stronger than you are." Dave rocked back on his heels, took ahold of her hands, and pulled her to her feet.

Now that they were both standing, they eyed each other cautiously. "I'll be right back." Cyd spoke first, inching her way to her bedroom.

Dave caught up to her and swung her around. "I'm pretty good with zippers and buttons. How about if I lend a helping hand?" He kept a firm hold on her shoulders.

"Let's not rush things," Cyd said with a strained smile as she pried his fingers off one by one. "I'll get into something I'm sure you'll appreciate, and then we'll take our time. We have all night to really get to know each other. . . ." Her voice trailed off suggestively.

Dave's hands circled her waist. "I want to be sure you mean what I think you mean," he whispered caressingly. His mouth was almost touching hers.

Cyd could feel the warmth of his breath as he remained poised for an attack. She, on the other hand, was hardly breathing at all. "Of course that's what I mean." She pulled away to give him an amorous smile, which she intended him to interpret as a promise of a sexual opportunity of a lifetime.

This one really got to him, and just as he was assuring himself that she wasn't his type. He was used to women who were finely polished, women who would never in their wildest dreams think about chasing down a man wanted by the law. Seeking composure, Dave took a step back to give himself some breathing room. He might be able to intellectualize away her appeal, but at the moment his body wasn't taking that into consideration.

Still working the same smile, Cyd slowly stripped out of her denim jacket vest and hung it in a closet. She had no idea if she'd be able to pull off her plan. It all depended on keeping him on ice in the living room while she got to the extension phone in her bedroom. "Why don't you just sit and relax?"

"I've gotten a little tired of the floor. I think I'll just stand," Dave answered, looking around the room. She didn't have a couch, or any chairs for that matter. At least not any finished chairs. Standing in sawdust in one corner of the room were six chairs she'd obviously been working on but hadn't completed. She was right when she said she designed unique pieces. From what he could make out, she was trying to create a cross between a butterfly and an octopus. There was a kitchenette off to one side . . . stove, refrigerator, cabinets, and sink. Again no chairs, or table for that matter. The apartment, as much as he could see, consisted of this one all-purpose room and obviously a bedroom, though the door leading to that room was closed.

"I use pillows. I'll get some. I don't like to keep them out . . . sawdust and all," she was saying as she quickly opened the closet where she'd hung her vest. She took out two plump navy-blue sailcloth-covered cushions and set them on the floor on either side of a cocktail table, which happened to be the only piece of completed furniture in the room. "Be right back," Cyd said in a singsong voice. With an exaggerated swing of her hips, she made her way to the bedroom.

His eyes were fixed on her shapely behind as she exited. Shaking his head to rid himself of all extraneous thoughts, Dave headed straight for the front door as soon as she closed her bedroom door. He had just turned the knob when she called out to him and asked, "Are you getting comfortable in there?"

"Very," he answered her. "How about you?"

"Oh, I'm getting very comfortable," Cyd responded melodiously, tapping her foot impatiently as she waited on hold for someone at the police department to take her call. Supporting the phone with her shoulder, Cyd began to unbutton her shirt so that she'd be ready to change quickly and get back to the living room.

On second thought, Dave couldn't see himself just walking out on her without saying a word. He had better manners than her boyfriend.

"I want to report—" was all Cyd got the chance to say on the phone to the police officer as Dave flew into her bedroom. He grabbed the phone out of her hand and banged it down.

"Don't you care that you might be sending an innocent man to jail? Do you want to have that on your conscience the rest of your life?"

"What do you expect me to do? Just let you go on your merry way?" She was getting very angry.

"I told you I was being framed."

"So you say. . . . Do you expect me to just take your word?"

He gave her a cold, menacing look. Cyd picked up her hair dryer, lying where she'd left it in the morning on the night table next to her extension phone, and waved it at him. "Don't you come near me!" she warned as he came close.

"Stop acting like an idiot. You know I can pull that

right out of your hand, and then we're going to go back to lying on the floor. Is that what you want?"

"What I want is for you to get out of here. . . . Just go!" she yelled, frustrated.

"I can't just go . . . and let you call the police. I'll never get the chance to track Hollis and Joe down."

"What are you planning to do . . . stay here?" This was all getting to be just too much, even for a woman like Cydney Knight, who planned to live life to the fullest, grab new experiences, let the cards fall where they may.

"I just don't know what to do," Dave muttered. "You really had me fooled. I thought you believed that I was telling the truth. Or at least that you were willing to give me the benefit of the doubt."

"If this were reversed, would you be giving me the benefit of the doubt? I bet you wouldn't." She confronted him squarely.

Dave contemplated her indignant brown eyes for a moment. She was right. There was no way he could see himself giving her the benefit of any doubt. He didn't bother telling her so. "Could I interest you in making a deal?"

Cyd put the hair dryer down, and then sat on the edge of the bed. The first four buttons of her shirt were undone. Dave figured she'd unbuttoned them when she came into her bedroom. Her shirt was no longer tucked neatly into her jeans, most likely due to their scuffling together on the floor. When she sat the shirt bloused away from her body just enough so that he could see that she didn't wear a bra.

She noticed the direction of his gaze and cast a dirty look his way as she rebuttoned her shirt. Embarrassed,

44

Dave turned and then took a walk around the room. He felt much better with every step he took farther away from her.

"What kind of deal?" Cyd asked after a minute or so of following his pacing with her eyes.

Dave stopped walking. "How about if I make it worth your while not to turn me in?"

"I'm listening." She'd bet this was going to be good.

"You said before you were in this for the money. How about if I offer you double the reward money if you promise to keep quiet and give me a chance to find Hollis and Joe and prove my innocence?"

"Are you going to give me the money now?"

"Don't you think it would be pretty dumb on my part to pay you up front?"

"Do you think I'm dumb enough to believe that you can lay your hands on twenty thousand dollars? If you had that kind of money to spare, you wouldn't be hauling wood for Griffith's," she threw back.

"Well, I do have that kind of money. Only I can't lay my hands on it until I clear my name. If I write a check or use a charge card, I'm going to be traced right here to New York."

"I have to hand it to you. You almost have me believing that you're being framed." She slid a measuring glance over him.

"What made you come to that conclusion all of a sudden? Is it that money talks?" He took a turn at being sarcastic.

"I've decided that if you really are a criminal, you would probably have hit me over the head by now and just beat it," she conceded.

Dave looked relieved. "I'm glad that's settled."

45

"But then again," Cyd said, "you could be just new at all this."

"Well, you don't see me lifting up any heavy objects now that you've told me what I should be doing," he challenged her.

"True." Cyd yielded the point.

"Then we have a deal?"

"I suppose so," she answered, still thinking it over.

"Why don't you give me your phone number? I'll stay in touch with you and keep you abreast of what is happening." He looked away from her with effort. Her sensuality—when she wasn't making a game of it— roused him more than he cared to admit.

Cyd got up from the bed and walked over to him. She raised her head to his. "You're smarter than I thought you were. Once you walk out of here, I know I'm not going to hear from you again."

"Has anyone ever told you that you are a very difficult woman to deal with?" Dave asked, annoyed at being pegged right.

"You have no idea how really difficult I can be," Cyd said with a cocky shrug of her shoulders. "Now this is my deal. I'm going to be your little shadow starting from this moment on. One way or another I am not going to come out of this a loser. If I get even the least suspicion that you've been putting me on about being framed, I'm going to turn you over to the police. And I'll find the way to do it."

"Terrific," Dave sneered. "And just how do you propose to shadow me all the time?"

"What do you mean?" She was stumped for a second, but then she got the picture. "I see your point," she

46

said, frustrated. She'd have to keep her eyes on him twenty-four hours a day.

Dave was feeling pretty good about setting Cydney Knight back a pace or two. She'd been trying to run this show. He had his pride, which was about all that he had left.

"The ball is in your court," he reminded her with a grin on his face as she stood glaring at him.

"I really don't want to even think what I'm thinking, let alone say it," she said tersely. "This is crazy even for me."

"Do me a favor then, and keep it to yourself. I've had enough shocks today to last me for a lifetime."

Cyd decided to ignore his condescending tone—and his advice. "All right . . . this is it. I will help you track down Hollis and Joe, and until we find them you will live here. What do you say?"

The correct answer to that question—the only sensible answer—was an emphatic *no.* . . . "Agreed," Dave responded after a pause. It really was the only solution. The way things looked now, he had to establish some sort of relationship with her. Staying close, he could at least keep reminding her of the money. That should guarantee her cooperation.

"I assume it goes without saying that the invitation doesn't include my bed," Cyd said sternly.

"You don't have to worry about me trying to get into your bed. I intend to keep my involvement with you down to a minimum. Lady, you scare me half to death. I wouldn't know how to handle you. You're too impulsive, too reckless, headstrong, and . . . and just plain ornery. Now, besides that, I find that you're mercenary as well. The only reason I've agreed to your deal is that those very qualities might just be what I need to help me find Hollis and Joe and prove that I'm innocent. Just so you know where I'm coming from, I intend to make you work very hard for the twenty thousand dollars I'm going to give you when this is over. Have I made my position clear?"

"Perfectly." She sized him up while she got ready to tell him another thing or two. Then she changed her mind and turned away. She wasn't about to give him the satisfaction of adding a hot temper to his list of her minuses.

Dave exhaled deeply, realizing he'd been holding his breath. "I don't know about you, but I'm starving. After dinner you can go with me to the furnished room I'm renting and help me pack my things." He was accustomed to making quick decisions and then acting on them. That was his secret to success.

"I hope you know that you are going to be paying half of the expenses while you're living here," Cyd said tightly. If he thought she was mercenary, he hadn't seen anything yet.

"That's fine." Restraining a smile, he studied her reflectively, knowing exactly what was on her mind. She didn't like the idea one bit that he'd told her she wasn't his type and taken away her pleasure of putting him in his place. "Look, I don't really like this solution any better than you do, but what do you say to the two of us trying to get along together?" Gentleman that he was, he offered her his hand to shake.

The nerve of the guy. Here he'd just about told her that he didn't like anything about her, and now he wanted to be buddy-buddy. . . . "Sure, why not." And

48

then, though it galled her to do it, she pasted a smile on her face and shook his hand.

He knew without a doubt that she was still fuming as he lead the way out of her bedroom. He stopped at the doorway and flashed a look back at her. She was still standing frozen in the same spot, mumbling to herself. "Come on, let's eat. I'm starving."

Cyd made a face behind his back. One thing was for certain. There was no way she was going to prepare that special French meal she'd planned for Josh. Leftovers . . . that's what she'd give Dave Bradley.

CHAPTER THREE

Dave washed his hands at the kitchen sink, following her lead. He was dying to get into a nice hot shower. His whole body felt as if it had been tied into one tight ball from his unaccustomed physical labor and all this tension, which was physical as well as mental. He might be able to deny it to her, but he wasn't fooling himself. As much as he felt certain that he wouldn't know how to handle a woman like Cydney Knight, he was dealing with a very strong temptation to throw caution to the winds and test his theory firsthand. The bottom line, as he saw it, was that if he let his guard down it would be much too easy to succumb to the attraction he was feeling for her. This was going to be one hell of an arrangement.

Cyd had opened the door to the refrigerator and was checking around the back of the shelves for the kinds of items you store and then forget you've even bought until they start to smell. Then it occurred to her that she would have to eat as well.

Dave leaned back negligently against the sink, his legs spread, and watched Cyd pull out a bowl of what looked like leftover chop suey. "That looks interesting," he said, feeling he should comment.

"Chicken stew," she called it, ladling the congealed mass into a pot.

"Recent?" Dave asked, knowing she'd understand what he meant.

"Within the last month," Cyd answered, favoring him with a sassy smile. She turned the flame on under the pot and went back to the refrigerator. "How do you feel about some warmed-over beets?"

"I hate beets."

"Well, then I guess it's no veggie for you tonight." Cyd closed the refrigerator door after taking out the beets.

"Would you mind if I take a look at what else you have in your refrigerator?" Dave straightened up and reached out for the refrigerator door.

With a bland smile, Cyd administered a light karate chop and dislodged Dave's hand from the handle. "You haven't contributed for the food, therefore you have no right to open the refrigerator."

"How much will it cost me for a look?" He crossed his arms in front of his broad chest.

"Do you want the price for only a look, or are you planning to feel around?" She could see he was amused by her quip.

"Why don't you itemize it for me, and then I'll decide what I can afford?" He grinned.

"Very well." She teased him with her eyes. "A look, no hands, will cost you ten bucks. A look and one quick feel will cost you an additional five. If you're planning to make a project out of it, I'll have to charge you by the minute."

Dave broke out into a hearty chuckle. "How about if I stand ten feet away while you open the door?"

"Tell you what"—Cyd broke off to laugh herself— "I'll be a sport. If you stand ten feet away, I'll throw in one look without any charge."

"Mercenary . . . that's what you are." Dave winked, then counted out ten paces from the refrigerator door. "I don't suppose you have a telescope that I can borrow?" he asked, stopping at the prescribed distance.

"Sorry," Cyd parried, looking at him impertinently. "Ready?"

Dave nodded and pretended to get serious, but he couldn't pull it off. He was smiling from ear to ear as she opened the refrigerator. Cyd counted out loud quickly to five, and then she slammed the door shut.

"I see you don't give much away," Dave said, pulling out his wallet from the back pocket of his chino pants. He slipped out a ten-dollar bill and waved it at her. "I'm buying a real look."

"Suit yourself. That will buy you two minutes." Taking the bill out of his hand, she stuck it in the front pocket of her tight jeans, wiggling a little to push it all the way down.

Dave's gaze slipped to the swing of her hips before he reached for the refrigerator door. He'd say this for her —she was certainly giving his power of resistance a workout.

Cyd walked up directly behind him and gave him the count. "One . . . one thousand, two . . . one thousand . . ." Pushing in front of him, she leaned back and closed the door. She started to laugh, then suddenly realized that she'd placed herself right smack into a very uncomfortable predicament. They were standing body to body, and Cyd didn't need any insight to know that nature was about to take its course. That hungry look in his eyes had nothing to do with his stomach.

Dave's heart was thumping. He was certain that she could hear it. Cyd, who was sure she could take anything in stride, was experiencing the same wild pounding in her chest.

"That wasn't very fair," Dave said, his voice catching.

Incredibly, she thought any minute now she was going to start trembling. That would be another first for Cydney Knight. "Sorry you feel cheated." She laughed feebly.

Dave placed his hands authoritatively on her hips and pulled her close. And then he did what he'd been wanting to do all the while he had her down on the floor. He crushed his lips against hers.

Cyd started to pull away. Dave tightened his grip, which, as it turned out, wasn't necessary. Within seconds she was doing her part. Her hands clung to his neck, and she was kissing him back with the same intensity that he was kissing her. Their tongues flirted with each other. She felt his hands move to cup the contours of her behind.

Somewhere from far away her common sense started to object. By the time she listened to it, her hips were grinding against his body, urged on by the demand of his hands on her buttocks. She shoved at his chest with all the strength she could manage. He let her go easily enough.

"That, I want you to know, didn't mean anything," she told him quickly, as soon as she was a fair enough distance away. "All it goes to show is that we both have active hormones."

Dave leaned back against the refrigerator to keep his balance. His feet had turned to rubber. "Whew . . ." He let out a low whistle. "I'll say this—I don't feel cheated anymore."

She was feeling irritable as hell. The look of satisfaction on his face wasn't helping any. She turned her back to him and focused her attention on the pot of stew. It was starting to burn. Cursing under her breath, she worked to move the chicken up from the bottom of the pot. "You're full of surprises," she said acidly. "I would never have expected you to have a cocky attitude."

Dave could feel his blood beginning to circulate normally. He took a chance and put his weight on his feet. "You know what they say about people who live together. . . . They start to act alike." If anyone had told him he'd become adept at one-liners, he would have laughed in his face. But here he was parrying with the best of them.

"Then if I were you I'd want to think twice about living with me. You don't want to go and catch all my other nasty qualities."

Dave grinned. It figured that she'd give back one better. "It might work the other way around. You might pick up some of my traits," he said, trying not to be upped.

"I doubt that I could ever be influenced to be gullible," she retorted.

Dave decided to let that remark go and quit while he wasn't too far behind. She was right. He had been gullible when it came to Hollis. Now, as he thought about it, he reflected that perhaps all his life he had been too much the romantic and not enough of a realist. It was a mistake he never intended to make again. "Can I do anything to help you along with dinner?" he asked.

"You can set the table in the living room. The paper plates are in the cabinet above the sink. The silverware is in the first drawer, in the second cabinet, to the left of the refrigerator."

"How about if we use real dishes instead of paper plates? I don't mind washing them if that's the problem."

"Very mundane," she told him mockingly. "Of course if you want dishes, you're going to have to pay for them as well as wash them."

Dave laughed. "I'll try getting used to paper. I think I'd better sort out my priorities before I go broke." He opened the cabinet, took out some paper plates, and then fished around in her silverware drawer. Apparently she didn't suffer from the compulsion to compartmentalize her utensils. Forks, knives, and spoons of assorted patterns were just heaped into one pile.

"I would suggest neatness as one of my traits worth copying," he recommended, walking over to the cocktail table.

"I'll reserve judgment on that one just in case you come up with something more appealing," Cyd sassed, following behind him carrying a bowl of slightly burned stew and hot beets on a tray.

He smiled to himself, privately giving her credit for a quick retort. "I don't suppose there's a possibility that you might finish up those chairs you're working on by tomorrow and maybe come up with a table to match?" he asked, folding his aching body down on one of her pillows.

There was a devilish gleam in her big brown eyes.

"You may not be in such a hurry when you find out there's going to be a rental charge for the use of a chair."

Dave slapped the sides of his pillow. "I think I can learn to like sitting on the floor," he laughed.

"Don't get comfortable. I want you to go start a fire." She gave him one of her dazzling smiles.

"Fire?"

"Fire . . . fireplace." Cyd pointed behind her back.

"Who makes a fire at the end of June?" He looked at her as if she were crazy.

"I do. That fireplace is the only redeeming feature of this apartment. Don't worry, I'll let you sit closest to the fan." She flashed another one of her winning smiles. Then, as promised, she got up and went over to the closet where she'd hung her vest earlier and took out a fan.

"You know I really do like to sit and watch a roaring fire," Dave said, placing some kindling wood on the hearth. "Seems we do have more than one thing in common. We both like a good fire and we both have active hormones to contend with," he teased.

It figured that he wasn't going to let her forget that kiss. "I, for one, am going to put my good old common sense to some use and make sure my hormones don't get the better of me," she countered.

Dave wondered if he could borrow some of her good old common sense. His hormones were acting up again. He'd let his mind wander over the way she'd felt in his arms and the wild, abandoned way she'd responded to his kiss. He'd had to tense the muscles in his thighs not to give away just how aroused he'd started to feel right before he'd let her go. Even now, just rehashing the moment in his mind, he could feel himself start to get all hot and bothered.

"I think while we eat we should discuss your problem," Cyd said as she spooned out some of the stew onto the two paper plates.

Dave held back a groan. She should only know the problem he was concerning himself with at the moment. "All right," he answered, suppressing a smile. Throwing a log on the fire, he came back to the table and carefully eased himself down to the pillow. She'd heaped his plate full of her stew. Spearing a chunk of what he hoped was chicken, Dave lifted the fork to his mouth. Thankfully he was hungry enough not to bother to savor the taste.

"Did you by any chance save the newspaper article?" Cyd asked, taking a taste of the leftover stew and deciding at the same time that she wasn't as hungry as she'd thought.

"It's in my suitcase. But I can almost recite it verbatim. According to the paper, a group of investors each received an offering on my letterhead. They were each given the opportunity to buy into a major shopping mall and hotel complex to be built in Honolulu provided they were prepared to act quickly. For a hundred-thousand-dollar investment they were each to receive a ten percent share. Since the men selected were all investors with whom I had done business on more than one occasion, and for whom I had secured healthy returns, they jumped at the chance to get involved. Of course they didn't realize that the pie being auctioned was far from legit. It probably says a lot for my reputation that only a few of them even bothered to call my office."

"I get it," Cyd jumped in. "I bet whoever did call

your office was told by either Hollis or Joe that you were presently out of town getting things rolling. What a scam!"

"A two-million-dollar scam," Dave said wryly. "I'm sure Hollis and Joe really put the pressure on those men to get their money in fast, warning them that they'd lose out on the deal."

"What about Joe? You said he was your accountant. He must have handled the books for other companies. I wonder if he did anyone else in."

"I called the companies I remembered Joe mentioning at one time or another. Not one of them had a bad word to say about him. I did find out, though, that he had mailed them each a letter recommending another accountant, advising them that he was relocating out of the state. I may be working on pure gut instinct, but I feel certain that the two of them are here in New York."

"We're really going to have to put our heads together to figure out what to do next," Cyd said thoughtfully.

Dave wolfed down his dinner. Sublimation, he told himself. He had the feeling that if he gave her half a chance she'd confuse his life completely. He forced himself to keep in mind that it would be stupid on his part to let some physical attraction get the better of him. So what if chills ran down his back whenever she looked his way. . . . He primly hypothesized that her bedroom probably had a revolving door. He told himself that she'd probably never felt one sincere emotion in her whole life, even though he didn't have any basis for that assumption. Her whole life, he imagined, was just one big lark.

Cyd put down her fork and pushed back a little way from the table. She brought her knees up to her chest and hugged her legs. Still deep in thought, she tipped her head to the side. The red highlights in her hair caught the glow from the log burning in the fireplace.

He caught her eye. She gave him a soft look with her cinnamon gaze, which he resolutely told himself was not as caring and sincere as it seemed.

"I guess we should go over to your furnished room and get you packed," Cyd said, stacking their dirty paper plates and the balance of the stew on the tray.

"Would you mind terribly if we put it off until tomorrow? I'm really bushed. I'd like to take a nice hot shower, and then hit the sack."

"Okay. The bathroom is through the bedroom. I'll excuse you from kitchen duty tonight. But don't think for one minute that I've gone soft. And . . . just in case you were thinking of asking, I don't scrub backs."

"I think I can manage, but I am glad to see that you do have a heart." He grinned. This was her game, he thought. She'd set the rules of conduct. He made up his mind to play it her way . . . all light, easy, and teasing. Actually it was fine with him, if for no other reason than it helped him forget the fact that the whole fabric of his life was in jeopardy if he didn't prove his innocence and clear his name.

Cyd smiled. "I have a very small heart. So don't press your luck. Tomorrow night you do the cooking as well as the cleaning up."

"Deal." Dave smiled back. "I may even splurge tomorrow and buy us each a real dish to eat off of."

"Don't go spending too fast. I just realized I'm going to have to hit you up for the cost of the wood you delivered. When I ordered it I was sure I was going to be ten thousand dollars richer."

"I guess I can swing it. I'll deduct the cost of the wood from the twenty thousand dollars I owe you. You're lucky I didn't spend all my vacation money. That's what I've been managing on until I get my first check from Griffith's."

"It figures that besides being gullible, you'd be frugal as well," she teased.

He swatted her behind with his hand as he took off for the bathroom. "Keep in mind that I could have thought up another way you could pay me back," he threw over his shoulder.

"Correct me if I'm wrong. But didn't you make a point of saying that I didn't appeal to you?" she called out to him. So, big deal . . . she was fishing a little.

Dave stuck his head out of her bedroom door. "It wouldn't have had much to do with whether or not you are my type. It would have had more to do with my active hormones."

She laughed. "In that case I hope you're planning to take a cold shower."

"Exactly what I had in mind," Dave bantered, saluting her with two fingers.

But Dave didn't take a cold shower. He adjusted the water to the hottest temperature he thought he could handle. All his aches and pains were back, begging for his attention. Smothering his body with the soothing warm heat of the spray, Dave waited for his muscles as well as his mind to relax.

He couldn't remember ever singing in the shower, but here he was using his baritone to the best of his ability. Since he preferred the songs of the sixties, he did a rendition of Motown's best tunes. He was working up a pretty decent imitation of Smoky Robinson when Cyd stepped stealthily into the bathroom.

She couldn't help noting the outline of his body through the frosted glass of the shower door. To her credit, she forced herself not to make a thorough appraisal, though it didn't take long for her photographic mind to click off a picture while she scooped up his clothes.

Dave stepped out of the bathroom ten minutes later with a towel tied around his waist. He looked at her sitting on the bed with her hands behind her back and a mischievous gleam in her eyes. He had no way of knowing that her look was very smartly covering a totally sexual reaction as she studied his physique.

Her first thought had been that he wouldn't make it through the front door of any Mr. America contest. But that wasn't a minus. She didn't particularly go for muscle-bound men. As far as she was concerned, Dave Bradley's tight, hard body had just the right amount of definition. She rated him a ten and she didn't consider herself an easy marker.

Dave smiled. "My first thought was that you took my clothes to have them cleaned and ready for me tomorrow, but I know better than that. Okay . . . give."

Cyd brought forth her hands and flung his boxer shorts at him. "I hid the rest of your clothing. I'm not taking any chances on you skipping out on me." Her eyes sparkled with humor.

"That's ridiculous. . . . We have a deal. Anyway, if I decided to skip out on you it's not going to be any trouble for me to wait for you to fall asleep and then hunt around for my things."

"I have a lock on my bedroom door, and I intend to

use it," she informed him impudently. "Now you can't blame me for not wanting to take any chances, can you?"

He was starting to get annoyed with this game. "I don't mind telling you that this is going to be a bit embarrassing for me . . . walking around in my shorts. Are you sure that won't present a temptation for you? I wouldn't want to wake up those hormones of yours again."

"You can take off that towel, and put your shorts on right here in the bedroom, and I promise you that I won't even be the least bit tempted to look." She covered her eyes with her fingers spread, letting him know that she didn't mean a word she'd just said.

"You don't mind if this time I play it safe," Dave laughed. "I'll put my shorts on in the bathroom. Do you think you might have a robe that I could borrow?"

"Certainly." Cyd stood up and went over to her closet. She pulled out a flimsy negligee she'd once bought but had never worn. She held it out to him.

"I think you'd do more justice to that than I would." He winked. "Perhaps you have something a little less risqué for me?"

"I should have realized that this was a bit too daring for a frugal sort of guy," she said playfully.

"Oh . . . now I get it." Dave grinned. "This whole act has been your way of getting back at me for calling you reckless, impulsive, and ornery. Well, let me clue you in. . . . If I were you, I wouldn't goad me too far. . . ."

She arched her brows. "My guess is that you're all talk." If anyone had come by to ask Cydney Knight what in the world was possessing her to flirt outrageously, she wouldn't have been able to come up with an answer.

"Do you want some action? Is that what you're asking for?" He knew any minute now she was going to back down, and so he wasn't surprised when she did.

Grabbing an oversized terry robe out of her closet, she threw it to him. "Here—you're off the hook," she laughed, deciding she'd been reckless enough for one day.

"You mean *you're* off the hook," Dave said, catching her robe with one hand. Probably she hadn't intended to let this routine go too far, but then again he wasn't positive. How do you like that? he thought, going back into the bathroom. Without even expending much effort, she already had him confused.

Cyd tried to control her laughter when Dave came out of the bathroom wearing her fluffy pink terry robe, but it got the better of her. He had to slap her on the back to cut her off.

"I'm sorry . . . but . . ." she sputtered as she stood up, and then she giggled once more.

She was starting to rile him again. "I'm so glad you're enjoying all this. Cydney Knight got in her last licks. Well, have a good night's sleep if you can stop laughing. I intend to spend the night dreaming up ways to get even with you," he snapped.

She stopped laughing and looked up at him contritely. "Are you mad at me?"

He looked into those big brown eyes of hers that played havoc with his senses and he melted immediately. Tilting her chin upward with his thumb, he slowly lowered his face to hers and placed a single light kiss on her lips. Then he smiled at her. The smile was

63

presumptuous and knowing. "I'm on to you, Cydney Knight. I think you're ready for me now—ready to put me in my place if I step out of line." Then, making a clean about-face, Dave walked out of the bedroom. Smiling triumphantly, he closed the door. If that hadn't been smooth, then he didn't know the meaning of the word. She could just think about that before she fell asleep. Suddenly he stopped short. . . . Maybe he should be thinking about that? Maybe she'd really wanted some action? Maybe . . .

Cyd sank down to the edge of her bed. She was feeling an emotion that had so far been contrary to her nature. She was vulnerable. More than that—for a moment there she'd felt practically defenseless. If she didn't watch herself, Dave Bradley was going to wrap her right around his little finger.

Dave tapped on the door first, then he poked his head in. "I was wondering . . . do you happen to have a folding bed tucked away in one of your closets? I'm starting to get an aversion to the floor."

He'd taken off her robe and was down to his boxer shorts. He'd been right about one thing. This situation was starting to be too much for her hormones. By the look in his eyes, she knew he knew it.

"You can take the mattress into the living room. I'll sleep on the springs. Tomorrow we'll see about making some other arrangements. Maybe we can buy a folding bed or something." Her voice came across as a schoolgirl whisper. A quick self-analysis was all Cyd needed to tell her that she was headed for trouble.

"Maybe it would be smarter to just rent one. I'm starting to go broke." Dave smiled softly as he took a few tentative steps closer.

Cyd turned her back, giving him an Academy Award-winning cold shoulder. Then she angrily ripped the blanket off her bed. He was right once again. It would be smarter to rent a folding bed. After all, he wasn't going to be here for long. He was going to be here only until he caught up with his ex-wife. That, she decided, was a very sobering thought.

CHAPTER FOUR

Dave was lying flat on his stomach, spread-eagle on the mattress. The single sheet he'd used to cover himself was crunched at his waist and twisted between his legs. Cyd stood in the living room looking down at his sleeping form and catching the full impact of his blatant attractiveness. She tried to keep in mind that all the men she'd ever met seemed to have some sort of deficiency. Either they were incredibly egotistical or lacking in sensitivity or just plain liars. The chances were Dave Bradley was one of the three or possibly all of the three. Not that it really mattered. She'd assured herself that she was over the idea of romance. Now if she could only overcome the unmistakable flood of sexual awareness that came from just knowing that they shared the same universe, she'd have it made.

Dave awoke only minutes later. His face was turned to the casement window, where some guy on a skateboard was bending low to look into the apartment. One of her many admirers, he assumed, getting back to his original premise that Cydney most likely didn't have the moral fiber to be true to one guy at a time. With a soft groan, Dave rolled over and shut his eyes. He counted to ten, then turned back to the window, opening one eye.

"Cyd, you've got company," Dave called out, clutching the sheet in an attempt to cover himself. The very last thing he felt prepared to deal with this morning was some guy bouncing in on him in a fit of jealousy.

Her bedroom door was open, but she wasn't answering. Dave slid off the mattress, keeping his back to the window. He wrapped himself in the sheet and sauntered self-consciously into the bedroom. Cyd was gone. Her bed, minus the mattress which he'd used, was made and his clothes were lying neatly spread out on top of her cover along with a note. Dave closed the bedroom door and picked up the note. After reading that she'd gone out to pick up something for breakfast, Dave grabbed his clothes and went into the bathroom to wash. He was feeling very pleased by her show of trust.

Cyd returned a short while later to find Dave gone. He'd left a note on the kitchen counter in which he claimed that he'd gone to pick up his things at the furnished room he'd been renting. She didn't believe that for one minute. He'd skipped out on her.

Without even stopping to think, Cyd lifted the phone and dialed 911, but before being connected with the police emergency line, she banged the phone down. Then she kicked the mattress on the floor, furious at herself for not following through with the call. Where was her good old common sense now, when she needed it? Placing the call at this point might still give the police time to head him off. Why was she giving him the chance to get away? She knew the answer, even though she would have liked to pretend that she didn't. . . . He'd gotten to her with those baby-blue eyes of his and that slightly off-center smile and the way he had made her feel that he liked her particular kind of crazy behavior. Cydney Knight was a naive idiot, and she was even more of an idiot now for not being able to shake off the effect he'd had on her. Disgusted with herself for not being able to turn him in, she kicked the mattress again. The thought that she'd been feeling more than just a sexual attraction distressed her more than the knowledge that she'd just lost out on the reward money.

His suitcase in his hand, Dave used the buzzer. He hoped Cyd had returned. He'd locked the door on his way out.

Cyd flung open the door and looked at him in shock. Then she snapped, "What are you doing here?"

"And good morning to you," Dave said, taking her ill humor in stride. "Are you usually this cranky in the morning? Or did you just wake up on the wrong side of the springs?"

She stood aside and let him in. All right, so she'd jumped to the wrong conclusion. That didn't warrant a smile, especially not while she was still berating herself for knowing what she knew now about her feelings for this man. Chances were she'd never turn him in regardless of the circumstances. And that confirmed her worst expectation. . . . She was starting to fall for him.

Dave walked into her bedroom and deposited his suitcase. When he came back out she was sipping something red in a glass with a band of ridges that had once secured a cover . . . jam jar, he suspected. With a smile, he slipped a five-dollar bill out of his wallet and placed it on the countertop. "You did mention something about going out to buy some breakfast."

"Help yourself." Cyd shrugged apathetically, gesturing at the refrigerator. He'd changed from the chino pants and white T-shirt he'd worn yesterday to snug-fitting gray cords and a navy cotton short-sleeved pull-over that heightened the blue of his eyes. He'd put together a dynamite combination.

"Cranberry juice?" Dave inquired, checking out her white sneakers, crew socks, pink striped suspender pants, and a hotter pink sleeveless cotton top. She put to rest the old adage that redheads should never wear pink.

"Tawny port."

Dave nodded his head. "Somehow I just knew there wasn't anything about you that was conventional," he said, trying not to notice the way the suspender straps of her pants just managed to skirt the nipples of her breasts. "I remember reading that some doctors recommend a glass of port wine a day. If my five bucks will cover it, do you mind if I join you?"

"It's covered. The bottle is in the cabinet above the refrigerator." She pointed the way as he favored her with one of his very special smiles. Though she gave no indication, a vibration ran down her back, a radiating reminder of her response to his chemistry.

The glasses, Dave found, were in the same cabinet. He chose one without ridges and poured himself a drink. He was having a hell of a time trying to read her this morning. She was definitely cool and controlled. He had a feeling she was angry, but he couldn't figure out why. She had said a polite enough good night before they'd gone to sleep. "Did you think I had taken a powder?" he asked after taking a swallow.

"It crossed my mind," Cyd admitted, tight-lipped. She wasn't going to mention that she'd nearly called the police. If she told him that, she'd also have to tell him why she hadn't followed through.

"Is that why you're out of sorts?" Dave persisted.

"What gives you the idea that I'm out of sorts?" She put down her glass and bent down to rummage through a bottom cabinet looking for a frying pan. In the process she extracted a paperback novel that had gotten caught between the top of the cabinet and a drawer. She also came across a deck of cards that must have fallen from the same drawer and landed in a pot. After having dumped out almost the entire contents of the cabinet, she stood up victorious, holding out a frying pan. "In case you're planning to remind me about neatness, you may as well know that I hate order and all other compulsive behavior."

"Being as sexy as you are makes up for all your vices." He gave her a sultry smile as he took the frying pan out of her hand and placed it on the stove. He didn't feel at all comfortable with her holding something heavy.

Cyd flew right to cloud nine on his compliment—not that she budged from her facade of frigidity. "Aren't you going to qualify that by reminding me that I'm not your type?"

He grinned suggestively. "Tell me about yourself, Cydney Knight. What really makes you tick?"

"Is that your way of saying you want to know more before you make a final decision on how to type me?" She smiled insinuatingly.

"If you don't want to talk about yourself, we can talk about me. I do better answering questions. So go to it."

"I don't need to ask any questions. I've already got you labeled," she answered briskly.

70

Dave smiled what he hoped was his most winning smile. He was determined to charm her out of her lousy mood. "While you're thinking up some questions, I'll start making breakfast. How do you like your eggs?"

"In the blender," she responded. "I took the frying pan out for you."

"Excuse me?" His eyes locked with hers for a long intimate moment.

Cyd took in a deep breath and exhaled slowly. Calmer now, she broke eye contact. "You make your breakfast, I'll make mine." Opening the refrigerator, she took out a container of unflavored yogurt and an egg. She selected a jar of vanilla beans from one of the cabinets and went to work.

Dave opted for a more orthodox meal of scrambled eggs, toast, and a glass of milk. He figured there was no point in asking her if she had any coffee. "There was some guy on a skateboard looking in the living-room window when I woke up." He spoke loud to be heard above the roar of the blender.

"Clyde . . . he lives on the top floor. We sometimes have breakfast together on Sundays. Growing up as an only child, I occasionally go out of my way for company."

"I kind of thought you did," he said sardonically.

Fuming, she switched off the blender. "This may be hard for you to believe, but sometimes, if I try real hard, I can have a stimulating conversation with a man and not think once of taking him to bed." Satisfied by his expression that she had succeeded in putting him in his place, Cyd marched into the living room.

She was spooning the concoction she called breakfast into her mouth when Dave joined her at the cocktail

71

table. They eyed each other as they ate. He was feeling like a total jerk at having implied that he thought she was loose.

"What made you come to Flatbush?" she asked after a while.

"Hollis's parents live in Sheepshead Bay." He was still privately admiring the way she'd told him off.

That made sense to Cyd. Sheepshead Bay was close enough to Flatbush for him to keep his finger on things. "Tell me a little more about your marriage?" she asked before putting down her spoon to take a delicate sip.

Dave concentrated on his plate, trying not to be distracted by her physical appeal. He wanted to achieve the kind of conversational tone she'd appreciate. "For the first four years I thought I was one of the luckiest men alive. She seemed happy . . . at least I thought so. I knew I was happy. Then one day Hollis sat me down and told me it was all over. She also said she didn't want to ever get to the point where she'd have to start acting in bed. I couldn't help wondering if that had already happened and my self-esteem dropped into the cellar."

Hollis, Cyd decided, needed her head examined. She thought of taking him right into her bedroom and giving his ego a boost. Biting down on her bottom lip, Cyd pushed the thought aside. "That sounds to me more like her problem than yours. I don't think most women would have to fake any response to you."

"I hope that's a personal observation." Dave smiled. To his surprise, he sensed a genuine concern for his feelings underlying her bantering tone.

"Theoretical." Cyd grinned. "But seriously, Dave, you aren't still taking Hollis's rejection to heart?"

He wasn't, he realized, reflecting that perhaps the reason he'd thought he'd had a good marriage was because the two of them had more or less gone their own ways. It seemed to Dave now that they had never really gotten to know each other outside of the bedroom. He hadn't considered it before, but there was even a chance that he'd married Hollis Logan more for snob appeal than anything else. She'd epitomized what he valued most—class with capital letters.

"Are you still upset?" Cyd repeated, studying his introspective expression.

He looked at her directly. There was a toughness and a determination about Cydney Knight that reminded him of the old Dave . . . the Dave that admitted to being born in Oregon but always left out that he'd spent his formative years growing up on the streets of Chicago feeling most of the time that he was trying to fight his way out of a paper bag. "My ego is still a bit fragile." He winked.

Cyd laughed. "I know any number of women who wouldn't mind giving that ego of yours a lift." She recognized intuitively that he was still internalizing his hurt. It was also obvious to her that he was determined to put up a cool and casual front.

"I'm a very committed type of guy. I wouldn't know how to handle more than one woman at a time. I think I'll just concentrate on you." There didn't seem to be any point in fighting it. He wanted to make love to her.

"I intend to hang tough." She picked up her spoon and waved it in the air.

"You weren't hanging tough in my dreams last night. I had all I could do to keep up with you. . . . You,

73

Cydney Knight, were absolutely shameless." He ended with his tone intentionally husky.

"Well, we can't always live out our dreams, and in this case that's a guarantee," she quipped, cracking a smile at her retaliatory rejoinder.

"It's a good thing," Dave said with a slick grin on his lips. "Do you think I want you taking advantage of me?"

"I think it's time to change the subject." She didn't feel as unaffected as she wanted him to believe. Her mind had latched onto the picture he'd started to paint and wouldn't let go. "Where did you meet Hollis?" she asked, uncomfortably aware that his eyes had settled on the rise of her breasts. She was breathing faster than normal.

"We met at college out in Berkeley and dated for a while." His gaze reluctantly returned to her face. "I was a senior and she was a freshman. Then after I graduated we lost touch with each other. Years later I ran into her when I switched attorneys. She was working as a legal secretary. The rest, as they say, is history. Now it's your turn. Tell me about yourself. You can start with why you got into the furniture business." He would have preferred asking her some more personal questions, but he decided to take it a step at a time.

"For a long while I ran the nine-to-five race," she began, genuinely relieved that they were back to talking conversationally. "Then one day I took a long hard look at myself . . . hated what I saw . . . and hated what I was doing. So I threw my hands up, remembered that I'd always thought of myself as being creative. I moved to Flatbush, number one because one of my girlfriend's aunts owns this building and was willing to give me a break on the rent, and number two to put more distance between myself and my father's concerned, but not asked for, advice. Before I moved here I had a small apartment in Manhattan that was close enough to his office to encourage him to visit quite a bit. Don't misunderstand me, I absolutely adore him—especially with him living in White Plains and me in Flatbush. Two hours is a perfect way of keeping the peace."

Dave laughed. "I understand perfectly."

"Anyway, since I've been in Flatbush I've taken karate lessons, singing lessons, and art lessons. I tried my hand at caricatures, but I didn't sell one. I've taken all sorts of part-time jobs to keep myself solvent while I continued the quest to find myself. Six months back I met this fellow who was a carpenter. He took me out on a job one day, placed a slab of wood in my hands, and taught me how to use some of his tools. This may sound crazy, but I get this euphoric feeling when I pick up a piece of wood and imagine it taking on an entirely different shape. I haven't earned very much yet, but I have gotten some encouraging feedback."

Dave smiled softly. "It doesn't sound crazy to me." He stole a glance at the chairs she'd been working on and he concluded that her designs were starting to grow on him.

She caught his appraising glance. "I'm very sensitive about my work, so if you don't like it, please don't tell me."

Dave reached across the table and ran his hand slowly and sexily up and down her bare arm. "I think you're very talented," he said sincerely. "I'm really pleased that I'll be taking a part in backing your venture."

She flushed slightly and hoped he would take it to mean she was pleased by his compliment . . . which she naturally was. But it was the feel of his hand on her arm that was raising her body heat. "All right, enough about me," she said, shifting away from his touch so that she would be able to concentrate. She'd had a thought a minute ago about how to proceed with his problem. As it came back to her she said, "When you were talking before about having met Hollis at Berkeley, I got an idea. You mentioned that when you call Hollis's parents that they hang up as soon as they recognize your voice. How about if I call and say that I'm an old friend of Hollis's from college and I'm trying to look her up? What's her maiden name?"

"Logan," Dave beamed. "That's a spectacular idea."

Riding high on his approval, Cyd got up from the floor and went straight to the phone. "What's the number?"

Dave had it memorized and called it out, digit by digit. Cyd let the phone ring for a good five minutes. "I'll try again in a little while," she said, hanging up. "There's another piece of business we have to take care of before we go any further." She walked over to her gray backpack hanging on the doorknob of the closet and extracted a brown paper bag.

"What have you got there?" He focused on the paper bag as she approached.

Her brown eyes were sparkling brightly. "This, my love, is the other piece of business that we have to take care of . . . and that's your appearance." She pulled out a bottle of black hair dye and a hair permanent kit from the paper bag.

Dave jumped up from the pillow as fast as a jackrabbit. "Oh, no . . . I'm not letting you mess around with my hair." He backed away as she persued him.

"What's the matter? Are you afraid that blonds have more fun?"

Dave continued to skirt her. "Cyd, I'm not going to let you touch me."

"Do you hear what you're saying?" She laughed.

"You know what I mean. . . ." He backed up against a wall.

"You're not going to be a baby about this, are you?" She followed along with him as he stepped sideways.

"Baby, huh?" Dave asked in a low sultry voice.

The intimate look in his eyes matched the tone of his voice. "Yes, baby," Cyd said throatily, responding.

"I'm not going to stand still and let you call me a baby," he said softly. But he had stopped moving and was standing perfectly still.

"What are you going to do about it?" Holding a package in each hand, she pressed her fists against the wall, keeping him captive. He didn't have any desire to escape. His hands crossed behind her back, catching her up in a tight embrace. Maybe, she thought, maybe she'd intentionally set herself up to be kissed.

"This is almost the way I dreamed it," he whispered, his warm breath against her ear.

"Is it?" she asked faintly. His lips were trailing down the curve of her neck, tasting her skin with the tip of his tongue.

"I think my hands were moving more like this," he murmured, pushing aside her suspender straps with his thumbs, then smoothing his palms down over her breasts. She glanced involuntarily at his hands and then up to his face.

"This isn't a good idea," she said breathlessly.

"This is my scenario, and in my fantasy you thought it was a very good idea," he scolded her teasingly. "As I remember it, you especially liked this." He candidly studied her expression as his thumbs erotically stroked her nipples taut. He could feel she was wearing a bra today, silky with a touch of lace.

Cyd was aware in the part of her brain that was still clicking that he was languorously building her need for more intimate contact. All his movements were slow and deliberate and designed to make her beg for more. This was the moment to stop him while she was still able to rationalize. Instead, her eyes closed. Her mouth parted for his tongue and she traded away thought for sensation.

He explored her mouth with his tongue while he explored her body with his hands. And just like the first time he'd kissed her, she felt his electricity from head to toe. Oblivious to the thump as the bottles she'd been holding hit the floor, she threaded her fingers through his thick blond hair and she kissed him back wildly.

Pulling away, he tried to get her blouse up over her head. Her suspender straps were in his way. She took the straps down and slid her hands through.

"Yes . . . yes," he groaned. "Undress for me, Cyd. I want to look at you."

She wanted him to look at her. She wanted to look at him even more. She started to unbuckle his belt. It was then that she suddenly realized that her hands were empty.

"Don't stop . . ." He was breathing heavily.

"Do you see what you've done?" She was looking down at the floor. The box containing the hair dye was

78

starting to turn black, which was a clear enough indication that the bottle had broken.

"I thought I was doing pretty good. You weren't complaining a minute ago," Dave said, his heart still pumping rapidly. He took a deep breath and then he raced for the roll of paper toweling she had hanging in her kitchen.

Giving him a crushingly sour look, Cyd grabbed a wad of the toweling from his hand. Dave bent down and worked with her to clean up the spill. The wood floor was already splattered with paint droppings. Dave didn't see that a few more mattered.

"Cyd, I do see your point about my appearance," he said in an apologetic voice. "The problem is that it's driving me up the wall to realize now that I have to sneak around as if I really were a criminal. I resent it . . . I really resent it. There are moments when I'd like to bury my head in the sand and pretend that nothing happened. I know one thing for sure. When I look in a mirror I want to be able to recognize myself. I'd rather try a wig, maybe even a fake mustache. That way I'd be able to take off my disguise before I go to sleep and know that I'm still me. Do you understand what I mean?" He followed after her as she discarded the bottle of hair dye in the kitchen trash can after wrapping it in yards of the paper toweling.

"I suppose you could give a wig and mustache a try." Her heart went out to him, which put her in a more precarious position than the one she was in already. The last thing she needed was some tender feelings. She was upset enough with herself for having asked for that kiss. "I think we should try Hollis's mother again," she said, more sharply than she'd intended. But before Cyd lifted the receiver off the wall, she turned back to face Dave squarely. "I may have asked for that kiss, but I'd appreciate it in the future if you would ignore any and all invitations. I sometimes act before I think."

"Sometimes?" he asked exasperated.

"All right . . . most of the time."

"Cyd . . . I don't think I'm up to handling this round. How about just dialing the number?" He didn't feel any satisfaction knowing that he'd been right from the start. She had him spinning in circles.

Cyd tried Hollis's mother again as Dave called out the number. Once again there was no answer.

"If you have a phone book, I'd like to see if there's a place where I can buy a wig," Dave said after Cyd hung up. "Then I'd like to take a ride over to Hollis's parents' neighborhood."

Dave found a men's hairdresser who advertised a large selection of men's hairpieces. They drove to the store and Dave purchased a dark-haired wig as well as a mustache that had been made up for a window display. Cyd was very much aware that Dave was not any less sexy-looking with dark hair than he was as a blond— nor was she any less attracted to him.

Hollis's parents had a classy address on Sheepshead Bay—an elegant high rise overlooking the water. Dave waited in the Griffith Lumberyard truck, which he parked down the street, while Cyd checked with the doorman. He wasn't as convinced as she was that the disguise made him hard to recognize.

"They're going to be away until Tuesday," Cyd informed Dave when she got back into the truck.

"I guess that takes care of that for the time being,"

Dave said. Dispirited, he banged his fists on the steering wheel. "I just don't know where else to turn."

"We are going to find Hollis and Joe," Cyd said earnestly, trying to cheer him up. "But since we're stymied for the moment—and I repeat, for the moment—what do you say to being a tourist and letting me show you the sights of the city?"

He stared at her questioningly for a moment. She really could be sensitive and caring. "I would love to have you show me the sights, but I don't think it's a good idea for me to be out on the streets if it's not necessary."

"You look so different, not even your mother would recognize you," Cyd said reassuringly.

"Maybe I'm just feeling too uptight today. Will you give me a rain check?"

She didn't dazzle easily. But every time he turned his extraordinarily blue eyes on her she melted. "I'll tell you what. We can go back to the apartment and you can watch me work. I did promise to finish those chairs I started by the end of this month."

"Could I hold the nails for you?" he asked, smiling now.

It was obvious that her idea appealed to him. "I'm giving you fair warning. If you plan on looking at me the way you are looking at me now, I'm not going to be held responsible for hitting your fingers instead of the nails." She was pleased that she had gotten him to relax.

"I'm glad that I do something to you," Dave said, lightly stroking her arm. "You do a lot to me."

"I'm going to do a lot more to you if you don't turn the key and start driving. I'll tell you ahead of time that you're not going to appreciate what I have in mind," Cyd teased gaily.

Dave grinned. "And here I thought my motor was already running."

Cyd reached across and turned the key for him. "Drive," she ordered, laughing.

"I'm going to buy you a fabulous dinner for letting me do all the dirty work," Dave joshed, opening a can of turpentine. He washed the brush he'd used to varnish the two chairs they'd completed.

"I always have dinner with my father on Sundays. It's sort of a tradition."

"You mean you're going to leave me alone to my own devices?"

"Not on your life. I'm taking you with me. By the way, do you have a suit?"

"I have a couple of suits with me." She had a funny look in her eyes that he found impossible to interpret. "I guess you dress for dinner," he said, wondering what she was thinking.

"My father tends to be a bit formal." She smiled a little enigmatic smile.

Cyd helped Dave unpack his suitcase after they finished cleaning away her carpentry tools. She even insisted on ironing one of his suits, along with a white dress shirt and tie.

Holding on to his newly pressed clothes, now on hangers, Dave followed Cyd to the bedroom to get changed.

"No you don't!" She laughed. "You are going to get dressed in the living room. I am going to get dressed in the bedroom all by myself."

Dave cocked his head and gave her an injured little-boy look. "You should be ashamed of yourself, thinking what you're thinking. I assure you I didn't have any ulterior motive in mind."

Still laughing, Cyd inched Dave out of the room. He heard the lock on the knob click behind his back.

He was dressed for a good half hour before he heard the lock being released on her bedroom door. Cyd stepped out of the room and Dave stared at her, speechless.

Languidly she walked around for his inspection, a mischievous smile on her lips. She'd zippered herself into body-hugging jeans of unpressed denim to which she'd added an army surplus shirt. The sleeves of the shirt had been cut off unevenly at the shoulders. Tipped rakishly on her head was a khaki cotton combat cap. Stopping in the center of the room, she slanted a look at him.

Dave took in the authentic military extras—a double line of World War II medals pinned above her breasts. It made no sense to him that she had told him to wear a suit to complement her look. "I thought you intended to dress up," he said, confused.

"I intended for you to dress up, not me. I wouldn't want to disappoint my father. He expects me to maintain my individuality." She gave him one of her saucy looks.

"Maybe I should change," Dave said. It was too mind-boggling to try to figure her out.

"Oh no." Cyd laughed. "My father is going to get a special kick at seeing me in the company of a guy who owns a business suit."

That sunk it. She was out to razz her father. The

contrast between the two of them really was comical. "Come here. I want to check your merit badges."

"You can forget what you're thinking. I don't have a medal for services beyond the call of duty." Giving him another saucy smile, she picked up his wig and mustache off the coffee table. "Don't forget to put these on."

"How about helping me?" Dave asked, clearly baiting her. The strange outfit she was wearing somehow made her appear sexier than ever. He couldn't remember a time when he'd wanted a woman more than he wanted her that very moment.

"Okay," Cyd answered, walking up to him and feeling the electricity as his blue eyes roamed over her figure. She liked the feeling. She liked it a lot.

Dave stood perfectly still, watching her as she removed the adhesive backing and placed the mustache above his lips. While she fitted the wig over his blond hair, he struggled to find something to occupy his mind other than the sexual magnetism sizzling between them.

"You're looking particularly handsome," she said seductively, looking him over with obvious approval.

"Is this one of those invitations that I'm supposed to resist?"

"This is one of them." She laughed, lying through her teeth. Cyd knew she wouldn't need too much persuasion to forget about dinner.

"Did you ever hear the story of the girl who cried wolf too often?"

"I have a feeling you're going to tell me all about it," she said, ushering him toward the door.

CHAPTER FIVE

"Daddy, this is James Portland, a new friend," Cyd was saying with a big smile. She'd come up with the name on the ride up to Westchester County.

Though Harry Knight recovered quickly, neither Cyd or Dave missed his look of surprise as they stood side by side. Dave gave Cyd a light pinch on the rear when Harry wasn't looking.

Daddy was one of those robust-looking men you picture sitting at a conference table mixing it with the shakers and the movers. He wore the aura of the self-made man proudly, and rightfully so, according to his daughter. Cyd had told Dave that her father had been a widower for the past ten years and in the last four years had become quite a man-around-town.

With shrewd interest, Harry centered his attention on Dave. He'd never known his daughter to go in for the Wall Street type before. "How about a cocktail before dinner?"

"I'd like one, Mr. Knight." Dave smiled. One scotch and soda later, the two men were on a first-name basis.

"James, what line of business did you say you were in?" Harry asked during the first course of a catered meal. He'd already given Dave a full rundown of his line of work—"the insurance game," he called it.

"I don't think I did say." During the ride over Cyd had offered a choice of covers for him to consider. They'd argued over most of them. At the moment he couldn't remember if they had finally agreed on one.

Cyd chimed in with an answer. "James owns a line of seafood restaurants on the West Coast. He's thinking of opening a few in New York." They were eating shrimp cocktails.

"How did the two of you meet?" Harry inquired of his daughter. In the back of his mind Harry started working up a sales pitch. He planned to interest James in a little New York insurance for his East Coast venture.

"That is really a funny story. Isn't it, James?" Cyd asked glibly.

"Very funny," Dave agreed with a grin. He was aware she was trying to get a rise out of him. "Why don't you tell your father all about it." He passed the ball back to her, knowing she was just having some fun.

Harry and Dave both gave Cyd their full attention. "Well, you see . . . I was at the lumberyard," Cyd began. Her eyes were playful as she singled out Dave's gaze. Suddenly apprehensive, Dave swallowed hard. "I was picking out some oak boards and wouldn't you know it"—Cyd paused to laugh—"right at that moment James was walking past me. Anyway, I lifted a piece to check for knots and nearly hit James over the head. The very least I could do was buy him a drink to apologize."

Harry shifted his gaze to Dave as he began to serve the main course. Cyd had called earlier to tell him she was bringing a guest. He'd ordered accordingly. "What were you doing in a lumberyard in Flatbush?"

"Browsing," Cyd answered before Dave could.

"Browsing?" Harry asked, wondering to himself if he could work that quirk in Portland's personality into a business advantage. Maybe James would like to browse through his insurance agency.

"Someone mentioned that particular lumberyard to me. I guess browsing around lumberyards is just one of the things your daughter and I have in common." Dave winked broadly at Cyd when Harry turned his head.

Harry gave them each a puzzled look as he sliced into his veal smothered in a lemon-based sauce. "I could tell you a few things about this daughter of mine—things I'm sure she hasn't mentioned."

Cyd kicked her father lightly under the table. "I'm sure James is not interested in hearing the story of my life."

"Oh, but I am," Dave said enthusiastically, tickled by the opportunity.

"Did she tell you that she gave up a perfectly terrific job and apartment in Manhattan to move to Flatbush to find herself? It was bad enough that she never wanted to work for me, but Flatbush? . . ." Harry continued, unperturbed.

Dave smiled. "She told me she hated the nine-to-five routine."

"I don't like the two of you talking about me as if I weren't sitting right here." Cyd flicked her eyebrow intimidatingly at Dave.

Harry patted his daughter's arm condescendingly. "Be happy that we're not talking behind your back. I could tell James about all your phobias, but I won't."

87

"What do you mean all my phobias?" Cyd asked pointedly. "The last time I counted I had only one."

"What one is that?" Dave asked, very interested.

Harry held his hand at the side of his mouth and tipped his head away from Cyd. "She's afraid of dogs," he said conspiratorially.

"That's it," she said, mildly aggravated. "I knew you were going to get to that. You can't stand it that I won't work for you. Why don't you also tell him how you're going to leave all your money to the ASPCA?"

Harry laughed. It was a running joke between the two of them.

"Why are you afraid of dogs?" Dave asked, smiling.

"Go ahead, Harry, tell him. I wouldn't want to deprive you of telling your favorite story." Cyd gave her father the floor as she finished the last of her veal and started on her noodles Alfredo. She really wasn't embarrassed.

Harry struggled to hold back a laugh. "When she was six years old I bought her a dog . . . not a puppy, mind you . . . but a full-grown Doberman. She picked him out herself. Anyway, Dusty, as she called him, had an eye for the ladies. He'd go chasing after every female dog in the neighborhood. Cydney wanted him to stick to her side. She was always one for commitment. Anyway, one day he got away from her when she was taking him for a walk. When she caught up to him she was so furious she bent down and bit him. Naturally, he bit her back. Of course we had to find another home for Dusty. He was as afraid of her as she was of him. Ever since then Cyd crosses the street if she sees a dog."

"You actually bit him?" Dave asked. He put down his fork and burst out laughing.

"I bit him, Dave . . . big deal." It was a funny story, but it wasn't that hilarious.

"Dave?" Harry looked startled. "I thought you said your name is James."

Dave stopped laughing immediately. He nervously ran his fingers through his hair, which was not his hair at all, but the wig. "Dave . . . James . . . she can call me anything she likes." Dave gave Harry a man-to-man nod.

Cyd sucked in some air. A wave of blond hair was peeking out beneath Dave's black wig. He'd just pushed it out of place. Sweeping her hand across the table, Cyd dumped the remainder of Dave's dinner in his lap. "Oh, I'm so sorry," she exclaimed, wide-eyed. Standing up quickly, she picked the dish off his lap and brushed off some strands of noodles Alfredo that were clinging to his trousers. After that Cyd took a firm hold of Dave's arm and practically lifted him off his seat. "We'll be right back," Cyd said over her shoulder, steering Dave to the kitchen. "I'll just help James clean up his suit and then I'll clean up the floor."

"I would have rather you bit me like you did that poor Doberman instead of dumping my dinner on my lap," Dave said in a teasing whisper.

"Cute," Cyd hissed, pushing him into the kitchen.

"Don't worry about the floor," Harry called out, staring after them. Trying not to excite himself, Harry leaned back heavily in his seat. What kind of guy wore a wig and wasn't sure of his first name? For that matter, now that he thought about it, Harry was fairly certain the mustache was a phony. Well, whatever was going on, it seemed clear to Harry that his daughter was in on it.

Cyd and Dave came back to the table. The front of Dave's suit jacket was wet. His wig was back in place. "Dad, we hate to eat and run; but James has an early morning appointment." She bent down with Dave and the two of them cleaned up the floor.

"You can't go just yet, honey. I have your favorite dessert. You know how you love strawberry short-cake." Harry was talking to his daughter but his eyes were glued on Dave. More often than not, Harry trusted his instincts. Right now his instincts were insisting that he find out what kind of guy his daughter had gotten herself involved with and why the hell it was necessary for him to be incognito.

"I forgot to tell you, the last time I had strawberries I broke out in hives," Cyd said, nervous now that her father would suspect something.

"I'll pick off the strawberries for you," Harry persisted. "And I'm sure James would like a brandy." Harry knew Cyd would not sit still if he started making "father noises." He'd have to play it cool.

"I do have to get going. I have some really pressing matters to take care of before I turn in." Dave shook Harry's hand and swung his arm around Cyd.

Cyd kissed her father lightly on the cheek. "I'll call you during the week," she said sweetly, and then she elbowed Dave in the ribs. She'd felt his pressing matter when she'd cleaned the front of his trousers.

"Cydney, I don't know why you bothered to come if you were going to just eat and run," Harry grumbled as Cyd walked Dave to the door.

Cyd stopped and blew her father a kiss before she closed the door. Staring after them, Harry was planning to make a few inquiries about James Portland. Better safe than sorry. His daughter didn't always use her head.

"I have a feeling that I just made a big mistake coming here. I'm sure your father realized I was wearing a wig. . . . He's bound to have found it a bit peculiar," Dave said as they started to walk. Playing it safe, he'd parked the truck four blocks away.

"I'm sure my father didn't give any of it a second thought. When it comes to me he's learned to expect the unexpected. You don't have anything to worry about."

"I don't know. . . ." Dave wasn't convinced.

"Take my word for it," Cyd reassured him, meaning it.

Dave forced himself to relax. "I still can't get over it. You really bit a dog?" He grinned, deciding to forget his concern.

Cyd laughed. "If you're going to tease me, I'm going to have to tease you back."

"What are you going to tease me about?"

"I'll think of something while we walk."

"Did you think of anything yet?" Dave asked after they were seated in the truck and he had started to drive.

"I could tease you about the look on your face when I first walked out of my bedroom dressed this evening."

"What look?"

"That look of stupefaction."

"That wasn't stupefaction. That was overstimulation."

"I'll grant you that you looked overstimulated a short while later, but at first you looked stupefied."

"Overstimulated," Dave maintained.

"Stupefied," Cyd repeated.

He reached for her hand. Without any coaxing, she placed it in his and squeezed lightly.

"I'm still feeling overstimulated," he said softly.

"Might I suggest a cold shower when we get back?" Cyd parried, making the same suggestion to herself. His overstimulation was catching.

"I was hoping you'd suggest something else."

"Animal," she quipped. Reaching out with the hand he wasn't holding, she turned the radio on. "What you need is some music to calm the raging beast in you."

The radio was full of static. Cyd fiddled with it for a while, then settled for the one station that came across fairly clearly as the truck sped along the parkway. She noted that he wasn't paying much attention to the speed limit.

Cyd flicked on the switch in the living room as soon as she closed the apartment door. She had the feeling she'd be safer in the light.

Dave looked up at the overhead light fixture and then directly into her eyes. "Who are you trying to inhibit, you or me?" He took off his mustache along with his wig. His eyes still on her, he shrugged free of his jacket. Then he moved in close. His hips against hers, he let her feel his arousal.

"Am I supposed to be turned on just because you're ready?" She tried for a sophisticated laugh as she took a step back, but it didn't fool either one of them.

"I think you are turned on. I think you're very turned on." He pulled her back into his arms. She didn't fight him.

"Egotist," she breathed against his lips. Not missing a beat, she linked her hands around his neck and kissed him long and hard.

92

He had his tongue in her mouth as he reached down to the hem of her shirt and slid both his hands up beneath it. She was wearing a bra. He felt around anxiously for the clasp, found it in front, and opened it quickly.

Cyd gasped with a wave of pleasure at the first touch of his thumbs on her already taut nipples. Her lips trembled against his, and then as his fingers played alluringly at her breasts she began to kiss him with a heat and force that elevated his already pulsating need.

"All I've been able to think about since I met you is this," he said thickly, pushing away in an effort to slow down his pace. He wanted to love her, not attack her.

He lifted her shirt up slowly to look at her bared breasts. She stopped him from lowering his mouth to her nipples for another devastating kiss. His fingers moved to the waistline of her jeans. She tightened the muscles in her stomach to give him more room, inviting him to move down lower. Ignoring the snap at her waist, he brought down the zipper. With a strangled breath, he slipped his finger inside and began to caress the silk of her panties.

Mindless, Cyd yanked at his shirt and his tie without making any headway. Her senses were centered on the maddening gyration of his index finger and not on her coordination.

"Yes . . . yes," he whispered to her. "Let me do this for you." He had all he could do not to rip her clothes off, but he didn't want to stop the pleasure his finger was providing for her as well as for himself.

Someone was telling her she had to stop now. Cyd realized that the someone was herself. She shoved

Dave's finger away just as she reached the brink of a climax.

Dave held her tight for a second, feeling her shiver. "I'll put the mattress back on your bed," he said hoarsely when she was breathing normally again.

Cyd watched Dave drag the mattress toward the bedroom. She didn't offer to give him a hand as he struggled to fold the mattress through the door. What was the matter with her? There was not one doubt in her mind that Dave Bradley was just out for what he could get. Well, she had news for him. . . . This was as far as she intended to go.

Cyd came up and leaned against the bedroom door. "I bet you never made love to a woman any place but in a bed," she commented idly, checking the clear polish on her fingernails. She'd had to grip one hand with the other to keep from shaking.

Stiffening, Dave stopped trying to straighten the mattress over the springs. He knew what was coming. . . . He had heard the slight taunt in her voice. It might not be visible to the eye, but she was carrying a bucket of ice water in her hand.

"I gather you don't care to make love in a bed," Dave said, lifting up her pillow from the floor. He punched it a few times in frustration before dropping it carelessly on the mattress.

"Not always," Cyd said remotely. No way was she going to let on that she wouldn't be able to say no if he came over and pulled her into his arms. She was using up every ounce of control just by keeping a safe distance away.

He gave her the kind of stare blue-eyed people do so well. "Would you rather make love on the floor, or how about the bathroom? If you'd prefer, we could even do it out in the street."

"I don't care to *do* it at all," Cyd retorted sarcastically. Anger helped. . . . At least it kept her from thinking about how much she did want him to make passionate love to her.

"Fine," he said dryly. The bucket of ice water she'd doused him with was even colder than he'd expected, but it did help to clear his head. Now that he was using his brain to think instead of another part of his body, he couldn't help feeling a little relieved. From what he knew about her now, he was sure she'd be looking for some kind of commitment. He wasn't interested in plunging into a relationship.

"Fine . . . fine," she mimicked him as she stormed out of the apartment. She was even angrier at him now because he'd so easily maintained his cool.

"Where the hell are you going?" Dave screamed, racing after her as she ran up the stairs to the second floor of the brownstone.

"I'm getting a folding bed for you," she answered bitingly while she angrily pressed the doorbell of one of the apartments on the second floor.

"What are you all bent out of shape for? You were the one who did the rejecting, not me." He really pitied the guy who would someday give his heart and soul to her. She'd probably stomp him to pieces.

"You didn't put up much of an argument," she fired back at him. She should have been thanking him for not bestowing on her some sugary promises—some tokens of love. In the state of mind he'd had her in, she might have fallen for any line.

"God . . . you are crazy. . . . You are truly crazy." He flashed a look at her as he paced around.

Cyd banged on the apartment door with her fists.

"Whose apartment is this, anyway?" Dave asked, staring at her.

"My friend Marisa Morano . . . Damn," Cyd muttered, turning away from the door. She just remembered that Marisa, an aspiring actress, was opening tonight in her first Off-Broadway show. "You can take the springs. I'm taking the mattress," she said acidly as she headed down the stairs.

"I had it in my head that maybe—just maybe—I could straighten you out," Dave yelled, following after her. "I give up. You confuse the hell out of me."

"Well, you're as easy to read as a book," she said, stalking back into her apartment.

"Read me . . . please read me," Dave challenged. "Maybe then I'll be able to figure you out."

"You want me to read you . . . I'm reading your signal perfectly clear. Wham . . . bam . . . thank you, ma'am. . . . Well, no thank you."

He looked into her big brown eyes, seething with indignation. What could he say? She'd just about summed it up.

The next morning Cyd and Dave could have posed for matching bookends. They were both in lousy moods.

"Do you want some?" She sounded bored as she motioned with her head to the pot of coffee she'd just made. On working days she always made coffee.

Dave was quite aware that the boredom in her tone was just a red herring. She was making an attempt to cover her anger. Well, he was just as angry. She'd done her share of flirting and coming on to him. He felt he'd been justified in expecting her to follow through.

"Thank you," he answered with as much pseudo-politeness as he could manage. Then he picked up the percolator.

"That will be a buck," she told him coolly.

Furious, he threw a handful of coins on the counter. "I'm only going to have a swallow."

She watched him carefully as he poured out a quarter of a cup. When she met his gaze they got into a staring contest. Neither one of them was willing to break eye contact first.

"I can keep this up longer than you can," he said goadingly, though he had the feeling he was going to crack any second.

"You're pitiful. . . . You really are pitiful." She drummed her fingers on the top of one of the counters while she continued to stare at him.

"Just so you know—I have to be at work at eleven." No matter what it took, he was not going to be the one to give in first.

"I can't believe you were dumb enough to take a job driving a truck," she sneered. Her eyes remained steady and so did the rat-a-tat-tat of her nails hitting the Formica.

"I didn't think you went in for status symbols." He glared at her.

She glared right back. "Dumb," she grunted.

"What's dumb about driving a truck?" he asked, infuriated.

"Ask the next cop who pulls you over and figures out who you really are. The way you drive, it shouldn't be long."

He let out an exasperated sigh. "I took the job because it provided me with some means of transportation, which gave me the chance to keep my eye on Hollis's parents' neighborhood. And the second reason I took the job was because I needed some money to—" He cut himself off. His mouth angled into a lopsided grin. "But you're right. . . . I do have a heavy foot on the gas. I guess it's lucky for me that I hooked up with you. Who knows how many other mistakes I might make? From now on I'm putting myself completely in your hands. What do you say? Can we stop fighting?"

She was turning to mush right before his very eyes, she realized. The soft smile on her lips was the first indication. Why did he have to know how to turn on the charm? Why did he have to be so damned sexy? "You'll have to tell Mr. Griffith that you can't work for him. You can tell him you've been called out of town unexpectedly, or whatever. Make something up," she said briskly.

"All right," Dave agreed. "But I still need to pick up some money."

"You can come with me to work today. I have to be in at two. I know Mr. Jensen is looking for some help, especially since he just got in a large shipment of shoes late on Saturday." She stopped speaking to study him quietly. "I don't apologize very well," she said after a minute or so. "But I am sorry about last night. It was probably more my fault than it was yours. I did lead you on. I guess what it all boils down to is that as much as I'm not your type, you're not mine either." Her type of man was one who would know when he was being offered more than passion and he would be willing and eager to make the same offer in return.

Dave felt a lasso circle his gut and pull too tight for him to breathe. He tried telling himself that her preferences didn't matter to him one way or the other. Why the hell should he care? "May I ask you just what type of man you're looking for?" he inquired, faking an air of nonchalance. He wasn't about to let on the effect her remark was having on him, but it was there in his blue eyes nevertheless.

"Now you wouldn't want me to ruin the start of a nice platonic relationship by answering, would you?" She winked at him, having already picked up that he had more than a passing interest.

Agitated, Dave restlessly rocked back on his heels. "Why is it that when I want you to talk you suddenly clam up, and when I wish I could shut you up there's no way of stopping you?"

"Women," she teased with a smile. "What do you expect? You can't live with them and you can't live without them. Come on, I'll take you upstairs to meet my friend Marisa and see if we can borrow a folding bed for you. I'm anxious to know how it went for her. She's an actress and she opened in her first Off Broadway show last night." Walking to the front door, Cyd had a bigger smile on her face than the one she'd shown him.

Cyd and Dave could hear a commotion going on inside apartment 2A. Cyd knocked, then turned the knob. Finding the door unlocked, she opened it and pulled Dave in with her.

"What's going on?" Cyd asked, looking from Marisa to the love of Marisa's life, her boyfriend, Luke Tracy.

"Do you know what he did?" Marisa screamed, not taking her dark Italian eyes off of Luke. Marisa went at him in her native tongue for a minute or so longer, and then she picked up a folded newspaper and read out loud, "If anyone in last night's audience swallowed Marisa Morano in the role of the Southern belle, then I'll start eating grits instead of mashed potatoes, and I'm a diehard meat and potatoes man."

"If you're going to quote me, then quote the rest of it," Luke said calmly. "I also wrote that it was a blot on the future of foreign diplomacy to miscast the dark-haired Latin beauty in a mishmash of a vehicle so ludicrously lacking not only a plot but sense of direction as well. But that's neither here or there. . . . I'm going to remind you one more time, Marisa, that you agreed I wasn't supposed to allow our personal relationship to influence me. There is absolutely no reason for you to be behaving this way."

Marisa was not giving any indication that she had heard what Luke had to say, possibly because she had heard it before. She began a new string of what everyone assumed were profanities in Italian.

"If you haven't figured it out," Cyd whispered to Dave, "Luke is a theater critic."

"Poor guy. He looks like he has his hands full with her," Dave sympathized, smiling at Cyd. Then he caught the look in Cyd's eyes. Before she opened her mouth to speak he knew that he had just inadvertently shortened her fuse.

"Sexist," Cyd lit into him. "Sexist . . . sexist . . . sexist. You make me laugh. You don't know the first thing about their relationship, but you're sure quick to put Luke in the right."

Dave gripped Cyd's arm tightly. "Don't we have enough to fight over without picking up on someone else's problems?"

Cyd started to pitch back a retort. Then, all of a sudden, she realized that Marisa and Luke were no longer fighting. In fact, from the looks on their faces as they gazed at each other, they were about to forgive and forget.

"You were so right, *cara mia,*" Marisa said, giving Luke the full benefit of a Southern belle drawl. "How do you say . . . ? That director was a mule's rear end."

Luke chuckled, drawing Marisa into his arms. "I need to give you a few more lessons in American slang."

"Hi, Cyd." Marisa smiled over Luke's shoulder. "Aren't you going to introduce your friend?"

"This is Dave. Dave meet Marisa and Luke," Cyd said. But by the time she was finished with her introductions, Marisa and Luke were no longer listening. They were kissing each other tenderly. "Is it all right if I borrow the folding bed?" Cyd went on, tapping Luke on the shoulder.

"Sure it is," he answered, breaking away from Marisa. "We won't be needing it. . . . Not for a while, anyway." He winked at Marisa. They'd been living together for the past month. Luke needed more than the fingers on both hands to count the times he'd been pushed out of Marisa's bedroom and had to use the folding bed.

The bed was set up in the corner of the living room. Obviously it had been used the night before. Marisa went over and pulled off the bedding. Dave folded the bed up for her.

Cyd poked Dave in the ribs when they were back out

in the hall. "I guess all's well that ends well," she said, favoring him with an engaging smile.

It didn't take much effort on Dave's part to smile back. Maybe what he lacked when it came to Cydney Knight was the power of positive thinking.

CHAPTER SIX

Ray Jensen, the owner of the McDonald Shoe Boutique —named for the street it was located on and not for any association to ground beef—was overjoyed to have James join his sales staff. Ray Jensen's female clientele were equally pleased. By eight o'clock that evening Cyd was ready to strangle the next woman who conspicuously hiked her skirt up higher than necessary to swing her legs provocatively at James, alias Dave. And only this morning she'd been congratulating herself that she'd talked Ray Jensen into taking Dave on because of the big shipment he'd received.

"Cyd, be a sweetheart and find me a pair of red pumps in a size seven for Veronica." Dave made a show of dragging his eyes off of Veronica's shapely crossed legs to look at Cyd. "I still haven't gotten the hang of the stock."

"Oh, James, I think I should go over the stock with you just one more time," Cyd answered in a honeyed tone, sugarcoating her irritation. Crooking her pinkie finger, she beckoned him over with a frozen beauty-contestant smile. Dave sauntered up to where Cyd stood, waving good-bye to Veronica. Cyd angrily flung aside the curtain leading to the stockroom. Dave stepped in right behind her, wiping a smile off his face. He'd been doing his best to make Cyd jealous.

"What do I look like—your slave?" Cyd asked in an angry whisper.

Standing tranquilly, with his arms folded, Dave eye-signaled to her to look over her shoulder.

Cyd glanced back and pasted another smile on her face for Mr. Jensen as he walked by balancing four boxes.

Dave waited for Jensen to walk out through the curtain. "Come to think of it, you look a little jealous to me," he answered flippantly. "You better watch that. I'm liable to get the wrong idea."

"Me—jealous? You should live so long." There was no way she was going to admit that he was right. That would have been even worse than having admitted the idea to herself.

On purpose, he fueled her anger with an insolent smile. "You could have fooled me," he said, looking her in the face. Satisfied that he had stoked her fire, he went on to say, "Well, whatever has gotten you so nasty, could you stop giving me such a hard time with each sale? I am really beat. I don't even have the energy to take advantage of the unexpected bonuses Jensen's customers are offering." He yawned and stretched to emphasize his recital. "What time did you say we quit?"

Cyd was so jealous now, she sputtered before she managed any comprehensible words. "In an hour," she got out finally. More in control, she added icily, "And you can find your own shoes. This job pays salary and commission and I'm not going to pad your sales."

"We're pooling our salaries . . . remember? I hate to say this to you, Cyd, but Jensen's customers seem to

104

prefer me to you. I wonder what it could be?" He couldn't help playing this scene for all it was worth. He liked the idea that she was jealous.

Ray Jensen came back through the curtain with the four boxes he'd just brought out and exchanged them for four new boxes. After thirty-five years of dealing with the public, the crease lines on Ray Jensen's face had formed a permanent frown. "Talk on your own time," Ray said tersely to Cyd. "James, you let Cyd feed you the shoes. I want you on the floor keeping the ladies happy." Making a stalwart attempt to transfer the lines on his face into a semblance of a smile, Ray Jensen walked back out to his customer.

Dave made it quite obvious that he was trying to contain a grin. "Red pumps, size seven," he said, brushing his navy slacks to let Cyd know that he was concerned about looking his best before he walked back on the selling floor. He was wearing the wig but not the mustache. He'd told Cyd that he was starting to get used to living dangerously. The truth was, the adhesive backing irritated his skin.

"I'd like to wrap a pair of shoes around your neck," Cyd mumbled to herself.

"Did you say something?" Dave asked, stopping at the curtain.

"I said I would like to wrap a pair of shoes around your neck," Cyd reiterated, inserting stops between each word.

"I'd be glad to accommodate you, providing you're wearing them." He smiled magnanimously while he waited for her to absorb his innuendo. He didn't have long to wait.

Her cheeks became inflamed and her eyes flashed

with fire. Muttering unintelligibly, she grabbed one shoe box after another from the shelf closest to her hands and started throwing them at him one by one.

"You can pay," Cyd said testily, sliding the check across the table. They had just finished eating hamburgers at the Black Fat Pussy Cat—an artsy-craftsy hangout on Avenue C down the street from Cyd's brownstone apartment. The underscoring of the decor was more on the artsy side than on the craftsy. White snips of paper announced each artist's price for a piece of his blood, sweat, and tears.

"It's not my fault that you got yourself fired." Dave grinned. "I'll tell you something. Jensen might have even forgiven you for hitting him in the head with a pair of boots if you hadn't gone to work with his price-sticker machine. It's probably going to take him a month to peal off all those stickers from the walls."

"If you hadn't kept dodging them, none of those stickers would have gotten on the walls," Cyd snapped.

"Well, honey, I think I'm worth more than eight dollars and ninety-nine cents," Dave laughed, digging into his slacks for his wallet.

"That's debatable." Cyd kept her tone down to a harsh whisper as she walked by his side over to the cashier.

Dave didn't speak again until they were outside in the street and had started to walk. "If you don't watch that hot temper of yours, you are going to end up a good-looking old maid."

"You can stick your predictions up your—"

He put his hand over her mouth, intercepting her just in time to smile at an elderly couple walking up within hearing range. Removing his hand before she had the chance to sink her teeth into his palm, Dave asked indulgently, "Could we pick up this conversation tomorrow? I'm too bushed to even think tonight."

"For two cents I'd like to—"

"Don't make me any more promises that you don't intend to keep," Dave said drolly, cutting her off again.

By now they were at the stairs to the brownstone. Cyd flashed ahead of him and rushed down the single flight to her apartment. Dave caught the front door just in time to prevent her from slamming it in his face. Still she made her point by slamming the bedroom door as loudly as she could.

He really was exhausted. All he wanted to do was lie down on that folding bed. Since he'd met up with Cydney Knight he hadn't had a decent night's sleep.

Just as he pulled the cover up and curled into a ball, Dave heard the TV in her bedroom being turned on full-blast.

"Could you lower that?" he called out irritably.

Cyd finished buttoning the top half of a pair of silk pajamas before she turned the volume up one more notch just for spite. "Put that in your pipe and smoke it," she retorted, getting into bed.

Dave tried clamping his pillow over his head. When that didn't work he yelled, "I told you to turn that down. I'm trying to sleep."

Cyd plumped her pillow up and leaned her head back to watch the eleven o'clock news.

"I'm counting to five. If you don't turn that TV down, I'm going to come in there and do it for you." Dave issued the ultimatum as he pulled on his trousers, hopping from foot to foot.

Cyd counted out along with him. Precisely on the stroke of five, Dave grabbed ahold of the bedroom doorknob and leaned in with all his strength, prepared to break his way into the room. He tumbled in rather ungracefully. She hadn't locked the door. He straightened himself up, still holding on to the doorknob. Then, handing her a sweetheart of a look, he walked over to the TV and turned off the set.

Calculating her moves, Cyd slowly unfurled her summer-weight guilt. Standing, she smoothed her flattering buttercup-yellow pajamas. After that, she stuck her nose up in the air and walked loftily to the TV. She turned it back on, adjusting the volume all the way up as Dave stood staring at her.

Dave reached over, turned the set back off, and then waited for her next move.

Cyd turned the set back on.

"Excuse me." His eyes were fixed on hers as he pushed the button back.

Firing him a look that was intended to kill, she pulled the button back out. "So sorry."

Dave whalloped her with his own version of a deadly glare before hitting the button again. Out of the corner of his eye he noticed that there was a pair of scissors lying on her bureau right next to the TV.

Treating him to a contrived aloofness, Cyd pulled the knob back out.

"I told you I'm tired and I want to get to sleep. . . ." Dave flashed her another look and turned the set off again.

"I know. . . . You're afraid you'll lose some of your appeal without your beauty sleep. I'll consider this a service to the women of Flatbush," Cyd yelled, putting the TV on once more.

"That's it," Dave said hotly, yanking the plug out of the socket. Grabbing the scissors lying on the bureau, he cut the TV cord in half.

For a long second Cyd looked incredulously at the two ends of the cord in his hand. By the time her eyes lifted to his face she was seeing red. "Now you've done it," she screeched.

He had a smile of accomplishment on his face. "I think if you admit that you're acting like an idiot all because you're jealous that a few of Jensen's customers were giving me the high sign, you'll be able to get to sleep."

"I don't have one ounce of jealousy in my whole body. . . . And if I was jealous, I wouldn't waste it on you." She didn't care whether or not that had made any sense.

"Whatever you say." Dave shrugged casually. "I know one thing. I'm going to sleep."

"No you don't. . . ." She grabbed his arm. "I can't fall asleep tonight without the TV, and if I can't get any sleep, you're not going to get any either."

Dave considered asking her how she planned to occupy him as she let go of his arm. While he waited to find out he found himself doing what he'd been cautioning himself against. His eyes strayed over the lines of her body. The slithery fabric of her pajamas just happened to be clinging in all the right places. To the best of his ability, he couldn't detect any line that indicated she was wearing panties, and he prided himself on his 20/20 vision. His hormones beat out his pulse as his entire system woke up. "I'll get you a new cord for the

TV tomorrow," he said, which was as far as he intended to apologize.

"That isn't going to help me tonight," she answered caustically. Her whole body was on fire from the obvious way he'd just toured her with his eyes.

"What do you want me to do?" he asked heatedly. The bigger problem was that he already knew what he would like to do. The kind of late-night entertainment he had on his mind might stand a chance of wearing her out.

"You figure it out," she said willfully.

Terrific, he thought, thinking again of what he would like to suggest. . . . Having her stand in front of him looking the way she was looking now was only making matters worse. It was too much for any red-blooded man. Dave was certain all this frustration had to be bad for his system. "I'll tell you what I'll do," he said, gritting his teeth. "If you get back into bed like a good little girl, I'll tell you a bedtime story." Little Red Riding Hood and the Big Bad Wolf came to mind.

"I don't want to hear a bedtime story," Cyd responded perversely. "I want the Johnny Carson show."

"You want Johnny Carson. . . . Well, Johnny Carson is what you are going to get. Now, please get back into bed." Sighing with relief, he watched her comply and cover herself up with the quilt. "Ready?" he asked.

"Ready," Cyd answered, hypnotically conscious of the small wiry blond curls forming a vee in the center of his nude chest. He was saying, "And here's . . . Johnny." Her gaze was shifting lower to where the tiny hairs disappeared in the band of his trousers. He was actually doing a Johnny Carson golf-club swing. Her heart was beating erratically as she fantasized finger-combing her way down beneath his pants. Admit it, Cydney Knight, the truth is you're going crazy wanting him.

"My first guest this evening is . . ." Dave paused to think.

Cyd motioned him with her hand.

"What are you doing?" Dave asked.

"I've changed my mind. I don't want the Johnny Carson show." After fiddling awhile with an imaginary dial, she settled back with a dreamy smile on her lips. "Now that's better. The late show is playing *Now, Voyager.*"

Dave studied her with amusement for a second. "Bette Davis and Paul Henried . . . Henried puts two cigarettes in his mouth and lights them both with one match. . . . It was considered very macho for the time."

"You do know the movie," Cyd said, surprised and pleased.

"Looks like we can chalk up one more thing that we have in common. I love the movies of the forties. I probably know *Now Voyager* by heart." There was a soft, sensual look in Dave's blue eyes. "Paul Henried stamps out both their cigarettes and pulls Bette Davis in for a kiss," he enlarged.

"I don't remember the scene quite that way." Her eyebrow shot up.

"Would you like me to personally refresh your memory." He was sure he could do a "mean" Henried with Cyd opposite him as Bette.

"Go right ahead," she invited.

Dave got ready to rise to the bait. Then he stopped

himself. Puckering up, he blew a kiss in the air. The lure she was offering smacked of revenge.

"Not enough feeling," Cyd complained naughtily.

"Just a minute." Dave grinned. He went into the living room and came back with his black wig. "I think the problem is that I need a prop." Holding the wig up in front of his face, he kissed thin air again.

"Henried would definitely have put more oomph into it. I think you'd better come here and try it out with a live prop." She met his gaze squarely, not certain at what point she had made her decision, knowing only that it wasn't spontaneous.

Dave stood rooted to the spot. "If I kiss you now, I'm not going to be able to stop regardless of how many curves you throw me."

Cyd tossed the cover aside and got up on her knees. She slowly unbuttoned the top of her pajamas. Looking into his eyes, she pulled her arms free.

"Cyd, don't do this to me." His voice shook. Not moving, hardly even breathing, his gaze fell to her bare breasts.

"I want to make love to you as much as you want to make love to me," she said clearly, watching a muscle work sporadically in his jaw.

He was at her side, drawing her up into his arms, even before he took his next breath. Groaning at the back of his throat, he kissed her hard, crushing her against his naked chest. When he raised his head she had a soft whisper of a smile on her face.

"Maybe you better try that one more time," she said breathily.

He did. This time he didn't rush it. It was a long, meaningful kiss. Strangely, he no longer felt the tense need for immediate personal satisfaction. Interwoven in his desire he found a mix of emotions he couldn't quite clarify. He only knew for certain that he had never felt quite this way with a woman before—at least not for years. It was almost as if he were anticipating the act of love for the first time, yet he knew he could rely on the maturity of discipline to love her in a way, he hoped, that she'd never been loved before.

Cyd sat back on her knees as Dave straightened up. He rested his hand on her breast and felt the rapid beat of her heart. He could hear his own heart pounding in his ears.

"I've been going crazy wanting you," he said with a shaky smile. To his surprise, he found he was trembling as he moved his hands over the roundness of her wonderful body.

She raised her hands to his shoulders, glistening now with a velvety sheen that made his muscles appear more pronounced. As she'd fantasized only moments ago, she raked her nails lightly down the center of his chest, thrilling herself with the thought of her destination.

He stopped her before she'd had the chance to open his trousers. She fought with him for a second. But her attention was quickly refocused on the sensations he was evoking with his mouth and his tongue at her breasts. She moaned aloud, arching for him, encouraging him to continue what he was doing.

She was breathing rapidly by the time he helped her off the bed and gathered her into his arms, her body molded against his, needing him for support. As their lips met his hands maneuvered down inside her pajamas, one hand in front sliding between her thighs and the other in back, over her buttocks. She was so hot her hips rocked turbulently, telling him in the only language necessary how ready she was for him. Cyd took the initiative and pulled her pajama bottom down. Then she pushed away to step out of them completely. Moving back up to him, she quickly unhooked his trousers, refusing to tolerate any additional foreplay.

"Not yet," he whispered to her. She could see in his eyes how torturous the wait was for him and she couldn't understand. She tried again to lower his trousers. He took ahold of both her wrists, forcing her hands to her sides. He leaned in and kissed her. His lips followed the contour of her throat, and then, down lower, over her breasts, over her belly. He let go of her hands to grip her hips.

She thrust her fingers into his hair. Her breathing accelerated as she opened her legs for him. He heard her sighs turn into loud moans, and in between her gasps of pleasure she cried out his name. He steadied her, holding on to her buttocks as she moved frantically against the demanding stroke of his tongue. He felt his hands were shaky again, even though he still managed to hold her tight. Nothing in his experience had prepared him for the overwhelming thrill that he felt just loving her the way he was loving her now.

She was moaning steadily—over and over again as her nails dug into his shoulders. Her body pitched, bucking against his mouth, and when she climaxed her ecstasy became his and he felt the satisfaction almost as if it were his own.

He stood up and held her close, soothing her caressingly while she continued to tremble. She spoke in a muffled whisper. He couldn't understand what she was saying.

"Tell me again," he prompted her adoringly.

"Please let me love you," she repeated in a stronger voice as she calmed down.

He closed his mouth urgently over hers. He felt her fingers glide against his heated skin. Dave had the sudden feeling that the intimacy they were sharing went beyond physical, beyond sexual. He had the feeling that she was reaching out and touching the core of his very soul.

Cyd lowered his zipper, and in one motion she pulled his trousers and shorts down together, helping him to free his legs. Then he stood there for her, letting her look him over. He seemed to be so much in control that for a second she was unsure of herself. She reached out to clasp him and he nearly jumped, groaning at her touch. And then she knew without a doubt how hard the wait had been for him.

Cyd dropped to her knees. Dave could barely breathe as he felt her doing wild things to him with the tip of her tongue. He thought he was about to go crazy and tried to tell her so. "I need you now," he said helplessly, trying to get her to stand up.

Her hands circled behind his back. She held him tighter, refusing to let go. Her lips moved more ardently as she became excited all over again just from the feel of him. By the time he did force her to her feet, she was as hungry for him as he was for her.

He practically threw her on the bed and just as quickly climbed over her. She reached down to guide him. It wasn't necessary. His urgency was the only direction he needed. Crying out her name, he lifted her hips and pushed himself deep inside her. Gasping and moaning, she wrapped her legs around his back. Her body moved with his. His pace and his drive were her own. She pressed up to him as their bodies whipped together faster and faster. She felt him carrying her to heights that she'd never even imagined possible, where nothing had any meaning except for the fusion of their bodies.

"Yes . . . please, Dave," she cried, shuddering.

"Baby, baby," he gasped, stiffening and then rocking with her in one final spin. They climaxed together, screaming out to each other in joy.

Dave fell over on his side, still gasping. When Cyd finally caught her breath she pressed her mouth to his ear. "Was it as good for you as it was for me?" Her voice was low and throaty.

He pulled her over his body. "Need you ask?" He nibbled on her lips.

She pushed his hands aside. "That's too vague. I want to know in your own words exactly how you felt moment to moment."

He grinned. "You're kidding, I assume." He took her face in his hands again and went back to nibbling on her lips.

She rolled off of him and sat up cross-legged on the bed. "I'm not kidding," she said, presenting him with a rounded view of her breasts.

"Where would you like me to start?"

"Take it from the top," she said, running her hand possessively over his hip.

"The top . . . Do you mean when you first opened your pajamas for me?"

"What were you thinking that very moment?" She stroked into place a wave of damp blond hair that had fallen across his forehead.

"Let me see if I can remember." Dave closed his eyes for a second while he smiled. Opening his eyes, he said, "I seem to remember thinking that perhaps I should kick in a little more money and fatten you up a bit." He wouldn't have been lying if he had told her that the very moment when she'd started to undress he had thought for certain that he had fallen in love with her. But now that the hot demand for sexual satisfaction had been appeased, he fought the idea.

Making a fist, she gave him a fast jab in the ribs. "If you're not going to talk sexy to me, I am going to go in the kitchen and make myself something to eat."

"Why didn't you say so in the first place? Actually, I'm starving." He gave her a teasing smile.

"If that's the way you want it." She swung her legs off the bed, trying not to laugh.

Dave sat up quickly and pulled her back down. "If you give me a minute, I'll do sexy things to you and talk about it as I do it."

"Are you sure you are going to be able to keep that promise?" She took a turn at teasing him.

"I don't know what in the world to do with you," Dave groaned, drawing in a sharp breath. Shocked, Dave found he was erect again even before she straddled him between her shapely thighs. He thought proudly that he'd just set a record for himself, though he gave Cydney Knight full credit for the incentive.

Cyd leaned over him and smiled mischievously. "Talk to me," she said.

He held both her breasts as she dangled them in front of his face and he gave each nipple a love bite in turn.

"The next place I bite is going to drive you into a

frenzy of craving," he said huskily, tumbling her over onto her back.

"New rules," she said, laughing as she fought playfully with him.

"What rules?" he growled against her hair after restraining her movement with his body.

"You have to stand over by the door, tell me what you're going to do, and then come over and do it," she explained, laughing.

"I'll agree only if I get in one freebie first." He grinned and stuck his hand beneath her to pinch her buttocks. "I love the way you move that beautiful behind of yours."

"You know what?" She wiggled against his hands. "We can talk later."

Much later, she curled up next to him, fully satisfied from their lovemaking. "I'm exhausted," she whispered against his ear. "I'm just going to close my eyes for a minute and then we'll talk. Remember, we're going to talk."

Dave smiled down at her before he rolled off the bed to look for the quilt he knew was on the floor. She was fast asleep by the time he tucked it over her. A second later he pulled the quilt back down, wanting one more look at her fantastic body. Then he lay down next to her, caught her up in an embrace, and plotted out a very satisfying dream. Cyd turned to her side, still lying in Dave's arms. She sighed deeply and tried not to evaluate her action but she couldn't escape from herself. She hadn't just made love to him. Oh, no . . . she'd given him her heart. . . . Only an idiot gives away her heart knowing beforehand that it isn't going to lead anywhere. Idiot . . . idiot . . . idiot, she told herself, praying it would make an impression on her brain.

Dave heard the shower running in the bathroom as he opened his eyes. He wasn't sure of the time, but the sun was shining against the single curtained window in her bedroom, sketching a pattern of light in the weave of the material. Stretching, Dave listened as Cyd turned off the water and opened the shower door. He couldn't help wishing that she had woken him up and invited him to take a shower with her. He had half a mind to drag her back into the shower. While he was still conjuring up the possibilities of erotic love scenes with the two of them lathered in suds, she stepped into the room. The first thing he noticed about her this morning was that she was fully dressed. For some reason that set off an alarm.

"The shower is all yours," Cyd said, not looking at him as she started across the room. She was determined to heed her own advice. The very last thing she was going to do was repeat last night's mistake. There was certainly no point in letting herself get hooked into thinking he wanted anything permanent. And if there was one thing she was tired of . . . it was being dumped.

The alarm tripped louder. "Wait a sec. . . . How about taking a second shower with me and then I'll take you out and buy you a nice big breakfast?"

"Would you do me a favor and drop the romancing? I think it's time we put all our efforts into concentrating on our financial arrangement."

"What about last night?" Dave asked tightly.

"I've already forgotten about last night. I don't think

119

you'll have too much trouble doing the same." On the tail of that remark, Cyd sailed out of the room.

Groaning under his breath, Dave got out of the bed and walked into the bathroom. He adjusted the water in the shower. Getting in under the steady spray, Dave realized quite suddenly that he was no longer upset by her change of attitude. Cydney Knight might want to pretend to herself that last night didn't mean enough to her to remember. He didn't believe her for one moment.

CHAPTER SEVEN

Dave placed a dollar bill on the kitchen counter and poured himself a full cup of coffee. "About that Pandora's box you opened last night," he began.

"What Pandora's box? What are you talking about?" Cyd asked in an annoyed voice.

"I'm talking about that very intimate high we shared last night. It's going to be quite difficult for me not to want another fix."

"You know what you can do about your Pandora's box? You can put a lock on it and throw away the key."

"Judging from the way you behaved last night, I think you're asking for the impossible, from both of us." Dave picked up the slice of toast Cyd had made for herself.

"I may have given in to my baser needs last night, but you can take my word for it, it's a rarity. I don't usually behave that way." Cyd grabbed the toast from Dave's hand just as he lifted it to his mouth. "You can make your own toast," she said as snippily as she could.

"Do you mean to tell me that you're not usually that passionate?" He intentionally misunderstood her.

Cyd threw the slice of toast down on the plate. "I'm not answering any questions. I don't even know why

I'm having this conversation with you." She picked up her coffee cup and walked into the living room.

Coffee in one hand, the slice of toast she'd discarded in the other, Dave walked right behind her. Cyd sat down on the floor, not bothering about a pillow. Dave laid his coffee and toast on the cocktail table and then went to the closet to get a pillow for himself. He settled down comfortably opposite her. "To get back to what we were saying," he started, after taking a healthy swallow of coffee.

"Watch my lips closely," Cyd said emphatically. "I do not want to talk to you—period."

"I get it." Dave smiled lazily. "I started off wrong. You'd rather I talk sexy."

"Aren't you listening?" she asked heatedly.

"Actually I was doing more admiring than listening." The huskiness he effected was only part make-believe. She did look incredibly good. Even in a baggy jogging suit that had seen better days, she had a certain panache.

"Maybe I'm not making myself clear. Last night I was suffering from temporary insanity. I am happy to report that I'm all cured now."

The sting in her tone would have made a bumblebee head for cover. Regardless, Dave plunged ahead. "Do you expect me to believe that if I took you into my arms and kissed you that you'd be able to stop yourself from wanting more? I think just thinking about it excites you."

He got what was left of her coffee in his face. Thankfully it had cooled down. For a second Cyd looked surprised as she watched the coffee drip down from his face and stain his white T-shirt. Then she ran into the kitchen for some paper towels.

"I am not going to say I'm sorry for doing that," she told him, helping him to wipe his face.

"That's okay." Dave smiled. "I'm not sorry for goading you into it. It makes me all the more certain that I'm right."

"Really slick . . . you think you're really slick. . . . Well, let me tell you something, buster, I can forget about last night just like that." She snapped her fingers for effect.

"I don't believe you," Dave said nonchalantly.

"Do you want me to prove it to you?" she asked without really thinking.

"Yes." He dared her.

Her head cleared. "Do you think I'm an idiot? There's only one way for me to prove that I'm immune to your charm."

"So there is . . . so there is." If he gave in to the feeling, her inconsistency could drive him crazy.

They sat facing each other, staring eye-to-eye. Cyd shifted her gaze. "Look, today is Tuesday." She brought up what had been on her mind since she'd wakened this morning. "Hollis's parents are due back. The sooner I try to reach them, the sooner we'll get a lead on Hollis and Joe. The sooner you prove yourself, the sooner you'll be able to get back to California." And that, she knew, meant the end of the beginning of their relationship.

She knocked the wind out of him. Here he'd been waiting for Tuesday and somewhere between Sunday and Monday he'd lost track of time. All he'd really thought about between now and then had been making love to Cydney Knight.

Dave checked his watch. It was nine-thirty. "Why don't you call and see if they're home?" There really was no point in trying to make head or tail out of what was happening between them until he put his life back in order.

Cyd got up and went to the phone. "What's the number again?" she asked tightly. She didn't want to understand the reason but she was feeling angrier at him now that he was concentrating on his problem and not coming on to her.

Dave got up and came over to where she stood. He dialed the number while she held the receiver. Cyd turned her back to him just in case he could read something in her eyes that she didn't want him to see.

"Mrs. Logan?" Cyd said into the receiver.

"Yes," Hollis's mother answered.

"I'm an old college friend of your daughter's . . . from Berkeley. I found I still had this number for her in one of my old address books. I was hoping to get in touch with her." Cyd turned back to Dave. He held up his hand, showing her that he had his fingers crossed.

"Really," Cyd was saying. "Then she's married. . . . An accountant—how nice . . ."

Dave was mouthing, "Ask where you can reach her."

Hollis's mother was already volunteering the information. "They're in Atlantic City having a second honeymoon," Cyd repeated for Dave. "I think I'll drop her a card. What hotel did you say they were staying at?" Cyd kept her eyes on Dave, studying the fantastic smile curving his lips. Hanging up, Cyd smiled back at him.

"Golden Nugget," she said, getting caught up in Dave's excitement as well as getting caught up in his arms.

"Do you know what this means?" he asked enthusiastically, swinging her around.

She didn't try to break away from his embrace, but her body was tense. "Now all we have to do is figure out how to get there quickly," she said, fighting the urge to run little kisses along the line of his neck.

"One of the smaller airlines must have a run." He let go of her to think. "We'd better figure on staying there. I'm not sure how long it will all take."

"Do you have a plan?" She leaned back against the wall. Her legs felt weak now that he wasn't holding her.

"Kind of . . . I have a few ideas rattling around in my head."

"It would be a lot cheaper and probably faster in the long run if we drove down." It wasn't as if she was head over heels in love with him . . . maybe head, but not heels. She was going to be able to handle it. . . .

"What about your car? What happened to it anyway?" Dave wanted to know.

"Don't ask."

"I'm asking." Dave grinned.

"Let's just say that we can claim it for a hundred bucks and a gallon of gas. I didn't get away with parking it in front of a fire hydrant."

Dave was still grinning. "Did you get yourself towed away by the police?"

"Bingo." She winked.

Dave slipped his arm around her waist. "The last time I counted there was two hundred dollars between me and the poorhouse."

Cyd smartly removed his hand. Dave chose not to

insist or comment. "I can come up with the hundred dollars to claim my car, but that's about it."

"We can always wash dishes if we run out of money." He swatted her on her behind. "Go pack a bag. And please do me a favor and change. If I can't touch, at least don't deprive me of enjoying a decent view." He gave her an exaggerated leer.

She threw up her hands in mock exasperation. "Give it up, will you?"

"Never," he answered as she skirted around him to walk into the bedroom. He followed, to lean casually against the door jamb.

"If you want me to change, you'd better get away from the door," she said, half smiling. All right, so she did like him coming on to her. That didn't mean she couldn't control herself.

"Why? You won't be showing me anything that isn't already imprinted indelibly on my mind."

"Get out," she ordered, starting to laugh.

"No. I won't get in your way. I'll just stand here and watch."

"I'm going to start throwing things at you," she threatened.

"I'll go if you promise to pack the pajamas you were wearing last night."

"I hate to dash your hopes, but we are not going to be sharing the same room in Atlantic City."

"I don't want to dash your hopes either. I am going to make love to you again."

Cyd threw her pillow at him. Dave caught it, threw it back at her, and then closed the door.

Five minutes later he knocked on the door, then opened it without waiting for her to answer. "I'm glad

126

you're not decent." He gave her a sultry look. All she had on was her bra and half slip. "I just remembered I'm supposed to work for Jensen today. I'm going to call him up and quit. I thought I'd tell him off while I was at it. Do you want to listen?" He wasn't talking to her face. He'd picked a different part of her anatomy to focus on—the part she'd covered with a bra.

She could just as well have been completely exposed for all the see-through silk cups of her bra covered. Cyd crossed her arms in front of her breasts. "You can tell me all about it after you make the call. Just be sure you tell him off good for me."

"I was wondering." Dave lifted his eyes to her face. "The first day we met you weren't wearing a bra. Since then you seem to be wearing one every day. I hope I'm not inhibiting you. . . "

"You don't inhibit me." Cyd went over to her closet and pulled out the first blouse she touched. She quickly slipped it on. "The reason I wasn't wearing a bra that day was because I had tried lifting weights with a friend the day before. I was in so much pain the next morning I couldn't twist my hands behind my back."

"Friend?" Dave asked.

"Friend," Cyd responded in an intentionally sexy voice.

"You can cut the act." Dave grinned. "I'm not the jealous type. Besides, now that you've met me, I know you're not going to ever want to look at any other guy."

"Oh, really?"

"Yeah, really," Dave confirmed, walking out of the room. This time he didn't bother to close the door.

"Egotist," Cyd called after him.

"You're slipping. You've called me that already."

Cyd came up and grabbed the doorknob. "I'll call you the rest of the names I have on my mind behind your back." Shutting the door, Cyd decided if she made sure to keep her conversations with him light and easy she might yet slide through this experience with her pride intact. There wasn't any reason for him ever to know that she had fallen in love with him.

It wasn't hard for Cyd to keep the bantering and teasing alive all during the time it took for them to claim her car and start out for Atlantic City. Dave was very clearly holding up his end.

"If you're hungry, we can stop for lunch at the next Howard Johnson that comes up," Dave said, breaking into the first lengthy silence between them.

"I am a little hungry," Cyd lied. The closer they got to Atlantic City, the tighter her stomach tied in knots. She had every reason to believe that whatever plan he'd mapped out had a good chance to succeed. Then he'd be hopping the first plane back to California. It was too bad he wouldn't be here long enough to see that she did have some rather nice qualities when she put her mind to it.

They hardly spoke again until after Dave had pulled into the parking lot in front of the next Howard Johnson and they were seated at a table.

"What was it like growing up in Oregon?" Cyd asked after the waitress walked away. She'd ordered a cup of clam chowder. Dave had ordered the same.

He thought about telling her some fanciful tale, but at the last moment he decided to be honest. "My family moved to Chicago when I was six months old. I grew up 'n Detroit, where my father worked off and on for Gen- al Motors—more off than on. Luckily my mother found work as a domestic. Little though it was, her salary provided most of the staples." He told her all this matter-of-factly, eyeing a picture of a landscape on the wall behind Cyd's shoulder.

"Who took care of you while your mother was out working?" Cyd asked softly.

"I kind of remember always taking care of myself. Though I suppose before I turned eight someone must have seen to my needs." He looked her in the face and forced a grin. Whenever he thought back over his childhood, growing up with a father who was a drunk and a mother who showed little interest in her offspring, Dave would find himself getting maudlin.

Cyd smiled tenderly. "How did you take care of yourself?"

"Let's see . . ." He studied her expression and smiled back easily this time. "Between eight and twelve I ran numbers for one of the local bookies."

Cyd interrupted. "Did you really?" she asked suspiciously.

"Not only did I, but I also kept a book of my own on the side—that is until Sam Maloney caught on and taught me a lesson about free enterprise."

She stopped him again. "Are you teasing me?"

"Would I tease you?" Dave laughed.

"Yes," Cyd answered, laughing also.

Dave waited to speak again until the waitress had served their cups of soup and their crackers and walked away. "I would never tease you about anything important," he answered sincerely.

"Why do I find that hard to believe?" Cyd shot him another suspicious look.

"Would you like me to show you the scar I still have

on my body from the beating I took?" he asked, giving her a wicked wink.

"I think I can say that I know your body pretty well and I didn't see any scar." She lifted an eyebrow.

"Babe, you got more involved with the front of me than my back. That's why you missed it. I'm quite willing to remedy that for you." He grinned.

"Eat your soup," Cyd groaned.

"I get it," Dave said, picking up his spoon. "You don't like talking sexy until after the sun sets. I'll try to keep that in mind."

The sun was setting by the time they walked through the double doors into the fantastic casino of the Golden Nugget in Atlantic City.

"Some place," Cyd said, moving closer to Dave so that he could hear her. The casino was noisy with cheers and loud conversations. In addition, bells were clanging on gold-colored slot machines.

"I have this strange feeling that we're being followed," Dave said, speaking just loud enough to be heard. He'd had the same feeling the last ten miles of the drive, but he hadn't said anything.

"Don't be silly," Cyd responded, looking up at the bubble-mirrored ceiling and knowing there were most likely quite a few eyes watching what was going on down below.

"Are you sure I look different enough not to be recognized?" Dave's shoulders were hunched up to his chin. He looked around stealthily, like a character out of a cloak-and-dagger movie. All he would have needed to complete the role was a trench coat. Instead, he was wearing a navy-blue sports jacket.

"Yes . . . stop worrying. Do you see them?" Cyd's

gaze moved to the row of slot machines and the line of people excitedly pumping handles.

"No." Dave sucked in some air-conditioned air, patted his wig, and tapped his mustache. "I'm going to find the desk and make sure they're registered." The lobby was right off the casino.

Cyd lagged behind.

"Coming?" Dave asked, stopping.

"I'll wait for you right here," Cyd responded, thinking of saying something like *I'll cover you*. But she wasn't fishing around in her shoulder bag for a gun. She was fishing around for a quarter. Those brassy-looking one-armed bandits were drawing her like a magnet.

The slot machine Cyd selected evidently hadn't been fed recently. It quickly swallowed up her first quarter and four more after that. She'd intended to risk only one quarter, get it out of her system, and then go back and wait for Dave.

"What are you doing?" Dave demanded, coming up behind her. It had taken him ten minutes to find her. A bellboy was standing at his side holding both their bags.

"What does it look like?" Cyd snapped. She was the worst kind of gambler. She hated losing, and that was why she'd never taken it upon herself to come to Atlantic City.

"Come on," Dave said, still on edge. "I registered."

"This place is really something else," Cyd remarked again, bedazzled by the glitzy decor as she stepped into one of the elevators with Dave and the bellboy.

"Hollis wouldn't have settled for anything less," Dave muttered.

They stepped out of the elevator at the tenth floor and followed the bellboy down a smoked-glass-mirrored

131

hall. Carrying both their bags, the bellboy showed them into one of the rooms. Dave tipped the boy before he walked out, leaving them with both suitcases.

Cyd knew the answer before she asked, but she asked anyway. "You did register for a room for yourself, didn't you?"

Dave didn't respond. He walked around checking empty closets, opening the door to an elaborately appointed bathroom before he sat down on the edge of a circular bed that was covered in the same heavy gold brocade as the walls and windows. He took off his wig and mustache. Now that they were alone he was starting to relax. "I know I said I would get us each a room, but it just seemed pretty crazy to stretch our finances." He gave her a much-too-innocent look.

"Well then, I hope you're not going to mind sleeping on the floor." Cyd stood with her hands on her hips.

"I thought if you were going to object, I would suggest that you sleep under the cover and I'll sleep on top of it. I think that's a fairly good compromise." His eyes teased her mercilessly, but deep down he was starting to second-guess himself. Par for the course, she did have him wondering if he was assuming too much. Was it possible that she was able to dismiss the way they'd made love to each other last night?

Keeping a straight face, even though she was amused, Cyd lifted up the phone. "This is room 1018," she said when room service answered. "My husband has been having some trouble sleeping recently, and since I don't want to be disturbed by his tossing and turning, could you please send up a cot?" Adding "Thank you" at the proper moment, Cyd hung up. "That takes care of that," she said with a sassy grin.

He tauntingly returned her look. "Now don't blame me if you spend the night going crazy because you can't get your hands on me. I don't want to hear about it." She wanted him as much as he wanted her, Dave decided, and he was just about positive about that—well, he was at least ninety-nine percent sure. . . .

"We should have gotten you a wig with an elastic band to stretch with your swelled head," she quipped.

"Honey, your head doesn't swell if you're telling the truth." He grinned.

"Are we going to play cat and mouse or are you going to tell me your plan?" She made an attempt to shoot him down.

"I think I'd better before I forget the reason I'm here." He stood up and lazily put his arm around her waist.

"I'm listening," Cyd said, swinging out of his reach. Why did her body have to heat up every time he so much as touched her?

"You remember when I went into the electronic store and you waited for me in the car . . ."

"Yes," Cyd said. "You went in to buy me a new cord for my TV."

"I also bought a miniature tape recorder. I have it here in my inside pocket." Dave patted the right side of his jacket. "The idea came to me in the store. I'm hoping to get Hollis and Joe to confess on tape."

Cyd smoothed down the skirt of her navy suit. "How do you plan on getting them to confess? Are you just going to walk up to them and ask them to speak into your pocket?" she asked flippantly.

He gave her a nasty look. Why was it that she could provoke him so easily? "No . . . I don't plan on going up to them and asking them to speak into my pocket. This tape recorder will pick up from a good distance, providing there isn't too much background noise. I just have to figure out a way to get them up here to our room to avoid having them call the cops on me before I get them to confess. Once I get them alone, I'm hoping that the element of surprise and the knowledge that I'm here and onto them will loosen their tongues. But first I have to find them. I hope they're going to stick to the casino in this hotel tonight."

Cyd's expression revealed that she didn't think too much of his plan. "How do you intend to get them up here? Do you have some sort of an inducement in mind?"

"I'll come up with something," Dave answered, annoyed that she wasn't impressed with his idea. He hadn't been able to come up with anything better.

Cyd sat down on the bed, rested her elbow on her crossed legs, and held up her chin with the palm of her hand. She was thinking.

"I suppose if I wait long enough, you'll come up with a better plan," he said, glaring at her. Her habit of being obstinate three-quarters of the time riled him to no end.

She ignored him for a few minutes, then said, "I don't know if this will work, but I might be able to get one of them up here . . . and possibly both of them. It all depends on whether Joe is the type of guy who is interested in a little extracurricular activity."

"Run that by me one more time," Dave said carefully. She had that look in her eyes that he'd begun to recognize. It meant she was planning something crazy.

"Joe romanced Hollis away from you," Cyd started off. "Wouldn't it be a kick in the head for Hollis if I try to romance Joe away from her . . . at least for the evening? Now I don't know if he'll go for me, but if he does I'll make sure Hollis sees me lead him up to our room. I'll bet money on the fact that she'll follow and blow her top when she walks in on her husband kissing another woman. Then, when the two of them are going at each other, you'll make your appearance. By then they'll be so off guard we're bound to get them to talk."

"I don't have any doubt that you will interest Joe, but did you stop to consider the possibility that Hollis might not follow the two of you? Do you know where that will leave you? That will leave you alone in this room with Joe, who is going to be looking for some action." Dave knew her plan had some merit, but he hated it anyway. He also knew why he hated it.

"No problem," Cyd said easily. "I'm going to be perfectly safe with Joe because you will get up to the room before we do and you'll be hiding."

"Where would you like me to hide?" Dave asked tightly.

"I don't know. . . . In the closet," Cyd answered offhandedly. She was still thinking over her plan.

Dave flashed her an aggravated look. "I won't be able to pick up anything behind the door."

"All right . . ." Cyd looked back at him, not paying any attention to his mood. "I know . . . yes, this is perfect. You'll hide under the bed. The bedspread will keep you concealed, and you can even lift a corner of it if you want to peek."

"Just for argument's sake, how long do you want me to wait before I rescue you from Joe's clutches? We'll have to give Hollis some time to follow the two of you . . . ten minutes, a half hour, whatever . . . and while

135

we are both waiting to see if Hollis does come barging in, what are you going to be doing with Joe?

"I can handle Joe."

"I just bet you can." His voice lowered dangerously.

"What's that supposed to mean?"

"Exactly what you think it means."

"I should have my head examined for even trying to help you." She angrily snapped open her suitcase.

"Don't help me. Do me a favor and don't help me."

Cyd took out her sexy electric-blue jersey dress. Holding it over her arm, she started toward the bathroom.

Dave swung her around. "You're determined to do this, is that right?"

"Yes," she said icily.

"I don't like your idea, Cyd."

"Why?"

"I think you know why."

Cyd smiled. She might be reading more into this than he meant . . . but where there was smoke there was also a good chance that there was fire. She straightened her arm, letting her dress fall to the floor. Then she brought his head down for a fast kiss. "That was not a promise of more to come," she teased. "That was only some reassurance that I know what I'm doing." She bent down and picked up her dress.

"I have a feeling I'm going to need a lot more assurance before this night is over," Dave said, calling after her as she scooted into the bathroom to change.

CHAPTER EIGHT

There was a fireworks display going on farther down on the boardwalk. Dave looked up at the moon and watched for another burst of sparks to light the sky. The humidity of the day had been replaced by a cool ocean breeze. There was a particularly appealing mix of aromas in the air—a combination of freshly roasted peanuts, popcorn, and Belgian waffles. Dave would have given anything to be able to enjoy the night, to forget about Hollis and Joe and the whole mess. He would have liked to take Cyd into one of the many clubs that lined the boardwalk and just dance the night away. She looked absolutely gorgeous in her electric-blue jersey dress. He felt miserable.

She felt tired—she felt depressed—she felt anything but good. They'd spent the evening hopping jitneys. They'd been in every casino in every hotel along the boardwalk for the past mile. Cyd knew how unhappy Dave was that they hadn't found Hollis and Joe. She would have given anything to put a smile on his lips.

"You are probably going to think I'm becoming paranoid," Dave said, swinging his arm around her shoulder. "But I am sure that man back there in the gray flannel suit has been behind us all evening."

Cyd turned her head to look back.

"Don't look," Dave said.

"If you don't want me to look, then how can I know who you're talking about?"

"You can look . . . just don't be obvious about it."

"I'll take a look around while I take my shoes off." The high-heeled strappy red sandals she was wearing were not intended for standing, let alone walking. Cyd gave Dave her slim red leather clutch bag to hold. Then, placing her hand on Dave's shoulder, Cyd slipped off her shoes and took a look around. There were quite a few people on the boardwalk taking a late-night stroll. She didn't see any guy in any gray flannel suit.

"Do you see him?" Dave asked, sounding agitated.

"We're both tired. Let's go back to the hotel and see if Hollis and Joe are back in their room." He was really getting distraught, she thought, keeping it to herself.

"You didn't see the guy in the gray flannel suit, did you?"

"Think about it, Dave. Why would anyone be following us? If someone had recognized you, you'd be in custody by now."

"You're right." He smiled faintly and turned his head a little to one side. He hadn't been good company all evening and he felt bad about it. "Did I tell you how fantastic you look?" He had told her but he wanted to tell her again. The dress she was wearing fell straight from her shoulders to just below her knees. It showed off her great legs and profiled all her fantastic curves. Dave had kept a pace in back of her more than once just to watch the movement of her trim derriere outlined in the fabric.

Cyd fingered the cameo pin at her shoulder where the material gathered into a cowl neckline. "You've already told me that you like my dress." She sounded sophisticated, she hoped. The last thing she wanted to do was let on how much his appreciation meant to her. It made her feel too vulnerable.

"I like what's inside of it even more," he added, smiling fully.

"Shall we go back to the hotel and see if Hollis and Joe are in their room?" She wanted the plan to work out for Dave no matter what it cost her personally. But what was she going to do when this was all over and he left? Her heart pounded in panic. She knew she'd never find anyone like Dave again. He was in every way her perfect mate, and she'd always remember that they were made for each other even if he never figured it out. Cyd bit down on her bottom lip to hold back a threatening display of tears.

"I guess we may as well." He took her shoes and held them in one hand. "I wouldn't mind carrying you," he whispered against her ear.

She smiled softly. "I think that would cause too much attention. We wouldn't want to do that."

He settled for slipping his arm around her waist. Remembering that he couldn't afford to bring attention to himself made him feel miserable all over again.

Cyd took her shoes back from Dave and put them on before they entered the casino at the Golden Nugget. They went straight through to the lobby and called up to Hollis's and Joe's room. There wasn't any answer.

"Let's go back into the casino and take one more look before we go upstairs," Cyd suggested. She wasn't anxious to be alone with him. There was no denying it—she was going to have a hell of a time trying to keep her hands to herself.

There still were more than enough people noisily trying to fill their fantasies at the gaming tables and the slot machines at one-fifteen in the morning. Under other circumstances Cyd wouldn't have been able to resist trying her luck at one of the roulette wheels.

"They're here. . . . I see Hollis," Dave uttered excitedly, tightly squeezing Cyd's hand.

"Where?" Cyd looked around.

"Blackjack." Dave made a jerking motion with his head in the direction of one of the tables.

There was only one woman sitting at the table Dave had pointed out so Cyd didn't have to bother taking an educated guess. Anyway, she had figured ahead of time that Hollis would be beautiful. Unhappily, Cyd noted that she'd figured right. Hollis was a study in white—white high-heel pumps—white slacks—white silk blouse—with white rows of pearls draping down to her waist—and to top it all a white Ivory Soap complexion. Cyd watched Hollis tuck her blond hair behind her perfect diamond-studded earlobes while she waited for the croupier to deal her a card, and Cyd wondered how many times Dave had run his fingers through those golden locks.

"Which one is Joe?" Cyd asked in a low voice, tearing her eyes off of Dave's ex-wife.

"Joe is walking up to the table right now. The guy with the crew cut. He's wearing a black silk suit."

And Cyd saw he was also blond and bronzed. There had to be something said for the California sun, even though Cyd decided to believe that Hollis had to do more to maintain the color of her hair than sit outdoors.

Cyd and Dave stopped walking when they were about ten feet away from Hollis and Joe. Dave turned, keeping his back to them.

Now that Cyd could see Joe up closer she realized that he wasn't as young as she'd first assumed. He had to be in his late forties, even though he was certainly making a determined effort to keep Father Time at bay.

"Tell me what they're doing. Is Joe sitting down at the table?" Dave was leaving it to Cyd to keep him abreast of what was going on. He didn't want to take a chance that Hollis or Joe would recognize him before he was ready to play his hand.

"Joe is still standing. He doesn't look too happy," Cyd reported. As far as she could tell, Joe looked like he was getting ready to take a swipe at his wife. They were having an argument. Cyd couldn't hear the words, but she could tell from their expressions. "He's trying to pull Hollis away from the table. It doesn't look like she intends to leave. . . . Oh, now Joe is walking away. . . . Yes, he's heading across the room. . . . I think this is a perfect moment for me to step in."

"Wait a minute . . ." Dave grabbed Cyd's arm. "We haven't gone over all the details. How will I know when to get up to the room?"

"Go up there now and wait," Cyd answered, keeping her eyes on Joe as he wove his way around the crowds of people at the dimly lighted gaming tables.

"I think it makes more sense if I keep an eye on Hollis. This way I'll be able to get a feeling of whether or not she's picking up on you and Joe. What we need is a signal so I'll know you're set to take Joe upstairs. I know what. . . . After the two of you walk through the casino, have Joe walk you to the desk. You'll ask if you have any messages. That will be my signal to get up to the room. To give me a head start, when you walk away from the desk drop your bag. Make sure you open it first so that Joe will have to pick up your things."

"You know what we haven't thought about . . . making sure Hollis knows our room number." Cyd couldn't help feeling nervous. The plan had more holes than a bucket of doughnuts.

"That's why you're going to ask for any messages. If Hollis is watching, she'll find out the room number from the desk clerk."

"But what if she isn't watching?"

"If I don't think she's picked up on what's going on, I'll wave to you from across the lobby and you'll say something to Joe about spotting your husband, and then you'll send Joe on his way."

"That sounds good," Cyd said in a small voice. Even though it was her plan, somehow Cyd didn't like the idea that Dave had figured out all the odds and seemed happy enough to send her off to play up to Joe. She still wanted him to be jealous of the thought of her in some-one else's arms.

"Remember, I'll be under the bed. . . ." Dave smiled wanly. "Try not to come on too strong to Joe. I'm going to have a hard time handling it. I don't know if I can handle it at all. . . . Maybe we should try and think up some other way."

Cyd kissed him lightly. She felt a lot better knowing he was still concerned. "Joe's not my type," she whispered, letting fantasy get in the way of her clear thinking. Nothing was going to come of her relationship with Dave. This was no time for any illusions.

"I'm still trying to figure out who is your type. . . ." He ran his hands up and down her bare arms.

"Hey, buddy, if you're not going to place a bet, then make room for someone who is." The guy making the request shoved his way in between Cyd and Dave, who were standing close to one of the roulette tables.

"See you later." Cyd smiled and then took off. The last time she had seen Joe he was stepping into the cocktail lounge that was right next to the casino.

Joe was polishing off a Chivas Regal neat, with his back to the bar, as Cyd walked into the lounge. He noticed Cyd before she spotted him. He had an eye for the ladies, and Joe thought this lady deserved attention.

Cyd caught Joe eyeing her and she eyed him back as she headed his way. This was going to be a lot easier than she'd expected. She walked right up and stood before him.

"Can I buy you a drink?" Cyd asked, doing her best to look sultry.

"Not tonight, beautiful. Maybe some other time." Joe turned back to the bar and signaled the bartender. You get married, Joe thought, and the next thing you know some good-looking dame with hungry eyes is interested in your company. There was no justice in this world.

Cyd pushed in next to Joe at the bar. This wasn't going to be easy after all—not that that was going to deter her in the least.

"Champagne, a bottle of Mumms if you have it," Cyd said to the bartender, catching his attention before Joe had the chance to place his order. Cyd felt Joe's eyes on her as the bartender nodded affirmatively. Cyd looked over at Joe through her long lashes. "Now

143

you're not going to make me drink the whole thing alone, are you?"

It took a minute before Joe answered. During that time he studied her appraisingly and came to the decision that Hollis was going to make a night of it. . . . Why shouldn't he?

"Let's get a table. I'll come back and get the champagne," Joe said, placing his hand on the small of Cyd's back to lead the way.

Cyd bit down on her bottom lip as she felt Joe's fingers spread open and moved downward. By the time they found an empty table his hand was nearly cupping her buttocks, and she was starting to inflict deep pain to her bottom lip.

"What's a beautiful woman like you doing alone?" Joe asked, helping Cyd into her seat.

"Trying to remedy that problem." Cyd ran her tongue over her sore lip in a way she hoped looked seductive.

"What made you pick me?" Joe asked, fishing for a compliment. He'd been propositioned more than once in his life, though not lately. Joe was glad the lights were dim.

"You looked to me like the kind of man who knows what it takes to make a woman happy." Cyd reached across the table to run her pinkie finger lightly along Joe's lips to make her point.

"Do you do this all the time? Pick up men in bars?" Joe dropped his hand under the table and rested it on Cyd's knee.

"Why don't I tell you the story of my life after you go back and get the champagne? A little bubbly helps me lose all my inhibitions." Cyd sighed with relief when Joe removed his hand from her knee and stood up.

She watched him walk to the bar. He looked like a peacock with his feathers spread. It was after Joe had paid for the bottle, while he was waiting for the bartender to get him a second glass, that Cyd looked around and spotted Dave. She tried signaling to him to get lost . . . that she was handling it. He was supposed to be watching Hollis, not her. Dave made a negative motion with his head, telling her he wasn't leaving. Cyd tried mouthing to him to go watch Hollis. Dave simply shook his head again, more vehemently this time. Cyd wanted to rush right up to him, throw her arms around his neck, and kiss him to death. She loved the idea that he was really bothered about her coming on to Joe.

"I told the bartender to make sure he put a second bottle on ice," Joe said when he came back to the table. He popped the cork before sitting down to pour.

"We never did get around to introducing ourselves." Cyd took a small sip. "So what's your name, handsome?"

"Bill," Joe replied. "What's your name, princess?"

"Princess," Cyd answered with a forced laugh. Joe responded with a deep chuckle. He put his hand out and squeezed Cyd's arm. Before he took his hand away he rolled his thumb quickly over her breast. Cyd glanced across the room at Dave. There was murder in his eyes.

"I like a lady with snappy answers as long as she doesn't speak in bed." Joe was still grinning.

"Is that where we're going?" Cyd kept reminding herself that she was doing this for Dave, even though

Dave didn't look like he was appreciating her effort at the moment.

"You move fast," Joe said, looking a bit thunderstruck. He hadn't really expected to score, nor did he have any idea how he'd be able to get away with it.

"If I'm moving too fast for you, then maybe I've made a mistake." Cyd spoke in a whispery voice.

Joe's hand found her knee again. Cyd hoped that Dave couldn't see what was going on under the table. "How about we finish this bottle up in my room?" Joe said, trying to map out a plan.

"I'd rather entertain you. Let's use my room." Cyd put a smile on her face. She'd never considered the possibility that Joe would want to take her up to his room.

Joe grinned. He'd tell Hollis he was going to take a walk on the boardwalk. He'd even give her some more money to gamble away. "Give me your room number and I'll meet you up there in . . . say . . . ten minutes."

"Either you come upstairs with me now or we just forget about it. I don't wait for anyone." She smiled to herself. She knew she'd scotched his plan to get by his wife.

"You are a demanding lady, Princess." Joe felt a bead of perspiration across his brow. There wasn't any way to get to the elevators without going through the casino. Was he really willing to take the chance on Hollis seeing him with this woman at his side?

"Is that a yes or a no?" She gave him an aloof look while she crossed her fingers. Cyd didn't want to think about what she'd do if he said no.

"Yes . . ." Joe pinched her thigh just above her knee. "Finish your drink and let's go." The hell with

Hollis, Joe decided. He probably shouldn't have married her in the first place. He probably wouldn't have if she hadn't dangled temptation in his face.

Cyd swallowed down her champagne and got up from her seat. Joe picked up the bottle. Cyd took a fast look over to where Dave had been standing. He was gone. She knew she could count on spotting him in the lobby.

Joe walked alongside Cyd but not too close.

Surprised, Cyd saw Dave in the casino. She wasn't sure what he was up to as she nervously watched him amble toward Hollis, who had switched from blackjaok to craps. Cyd changed her direction and made sure she was walking close to the table where Hollis was playing. She slowed her pace, forcing Joe to do so. Joe, Cyd noted, had his hand at the side of his face, trying to keep from being noticed.

"Why are you holding your hand up to your face? Are you hiding from someone?" Cyd asked pointedly. Joe Thomas was more transparent than Saran Wrap.

"I've got a tooth that acts up now and then. It's better now." For a minute Joe looked like he didn't know what to do with his hand. He slapped his jaw, his chin, and then finally used it to grab Cyd by the elbow. He tried to steer her in a different direction.

Cyd stopped walking, bringing Joe up short. "Shall we try our luck with the dice before we go upstairs?" Her bravado about being able to handle Joe was slipping—no, *slipping* was not quite the word. It had just about evaporated. . . .

"You've got me warmed, Princess. You don't want to cool me down." Joe pushed Cyd ahead and forced himself not to look to see if Hollis had noticed him.

"Right," Cyd said, nearly choking on the word.

"Damn if that don't look like my wife with that stud-looking guy," Dave was saying to some guy standing at Hollis's side. He had his fingers crossed that his remark would catch his ex-wife's interest. Dave knew he was taking a big risk that Hollis might look at him squarely and recognize him in his disguise, but he had no choice. He knew she hadn't noticed Cyd and Joe.

For a split second Hollis looked at Dave, but by then he had averted his face, and then she turned her head in the direction of his gaze. That's when her mouth dropped open. The stud with this guy's wife was her husband.

"Lady, you going to throw those dice?" one of the other men at the table called over to Hollis. She was clutching the dice in her fist and staring after Cyd and Joe as they headed out of the casino.

Fuming, Hollis flung the dice across the table.

"Sixes," the croupier called out. "The lady is a winner again."

By now Cyd and Joe were out in the lobby. Dave was rushing out of the casino not too far in back of them. "I just want to check at the desk and see if I have any messages," Cyd said to Joe while she asked herself, *When am I going to learn to keep my mouth shut?* She wasn't at all happy to be carrying out her own plan to seduce Joe.

"Can't you do that later?" Joe said, wiping his brow before he took a firm hold of Cyd's arm and tried to steer her toward the elevators.

Cyd peeled his arm away. "I'm starting to have second thoughts. . . . I don't care to be rushed," she said before walking off toward the desk. She was starting to worry that Dave wouldn't catch up to them in time and get up to the room before they did.

"Who said anything about rushing, Princess?" was Joe's answer as he hurried after her.

Luck was on her side. There was still a beehive of activity going on at the desk. Check-ins and checkouts were handled around the clock. Cyd stole a look around for Dave as she waited for a clerk. With relief, she saw Dave standing near the bank of elevators. He winked at her as one of the doors opened. Then he stepped inside.

Cyd looked back at the casino and caught sight of Hollis surreptitiously watching them. Hollis turned away as soon as Joe followed the direction of Cyd's gaze, but Joe saw the back of his wife and froze. Cyd panicked. One of two things could happen. Joe could change his mind or Hollis could confront them before she got Joe up to the room.

"I'll wait for you by the elevator," Joe said, making a decision to put some distance between himself and the Princess. If nothing else, he intended to play it cagey. If Hollis walked out of the casino and saw him, she'd see him standing alone.

Cyd was quick to realize Joe's plan fell in with hers and so she nodded agreeably. Now all she had to do was make sure she mentioned their room number to one of the clerks and then pray that Hollis would come up and ask for it once she got Joe up to the room.

"Are there any messages for room 1018?" Cyd asked, finally getting a clerk's attention.

The clerk turned to a slotted wall to check. "There isn't anything here for room 1018," he answered.

"Are you sure . . . room 1018?" Cyd repeated.

"Nothing," the clerk answered without looking.

Cyd walked across the lobby to Joe, who was pretending he didn't know her. Cyd was determined to remind him for Hollis's benefit, but just as she started to put her arm around him the elevator door opened and Joe rushed in. . . . Still Cyd managed to pat him playfully on the behind before the door closed.

Hollis stood in the lobby, still giving the closed elevator door a long look. She couldn't believe her eyes. That was her husband whose rear end had just been tapped.

Hollis walked quickly over to the desk. She had less trouble than Cyd had had getting a clerk's attention. It could have been because of the fire in her green eyes.

"I want to talk to that man over there." Hollis pointed to the clerk who had spoken with Cyd.

"Are you a guest?" she was asked.

"Yes . . . I'm a guest, and if you don't tell that guy over there that I want to speak to him I'm going to let everyone in the lobby know what kind of hotel you are running."

The clerk she wanted was summoned and came up to her on the double. "Can I help you?" he asked, feeling hostile. He really resented people who got irate over some minor inconvenience. She was probably going to make a big stink about missing some towels in her bathroom. Although why she'd singled him out was beyond him. He'd probably been the lucky one to check her into the hotel.

"That woman you were just speaking to . . . the one in the blue dress . . . red hair . . . is she registered?" Hollis didn't believe Joe would be stupid enough to take a woman up to their room, but then again . . .

"She's registered," the clerk replied shortly.

"What's her room number?" The clerk didn't look like he was about to tell her so Hollis put on a sweetie-pie smile. "We're old friends. I haven't seen her in years. She's going to be real happy to see me."

"1018," the clerk said indifferently and then went about his business.

Hollis started for the elevators and then stopped. If Joe was up to something, she intended to catch him with his pants down, and she meant that literally. Making a smooth about-face, Hollis marched over to one of the rows of slot machines in the lobby. She intended to give Joe just enough time to incriminate himself.

Cyd had walked into the bathroom. She came out carrying the two glasses the management supplied. Joe was taking off his jacket and tie. Dave was under the bed holding his tape recorder.

"I hate to go to bed with men who are perfect strangers." Cyd forced a smile as she held out both glasses. "Tell me a little about yourself."

Joe poured the champagne, finishing off the bottle. "What kind of things would you like to know?" He decided he'd give her ten minutes. If she wasn't undressed by then, he was walking out.

"You look like a man of means . . ." Cyd fingered his pure silk shirt. "What do you do for a living?"

"I'm an accountant," Joe answered, wishing the champagne he was drinking offered more of a buzz. He was feeling tense.

"I didn't realize accountants did so well. I bet you have something else going for you on the side." Cyd smiled a bit more naturally.

Dave smiled also as he lay under the bed. Cyd was

151

really fantastic, he thought, mentally applauding the way she was trying to set Joe up.

"Well, I do a little of this and a little of that." Joe put down his glass and then took Cyd's glass out of her hand.

"What exactly does a little of this and a little of that mean?" Cyd moved back a step.

Joe stopped in his tracks. "Hey, is this going to cost me? If it is, I'm not buying." He reached for his jacket. He'd thrown it on the bed.

"I'm not selling, handsome." Cyd took his jacket out of his hand and dropped it to the floor. Where the hell was Hollis? she wondered.

Dave was wondering the same thing until he felt the springs bounce over his body. Then all he could think about was what was happening on top of the bed.

"Hey, handsome," Cyd said, struggling to push him off of her body. "I told you I don't like to be rushed."

"Listen, Princess, either you start showing me that it was worth my while coming up here or I'm leaving," Joe said flatly, breathing down on her face.

"If you get off of me, I'll get undressed," Cyd responded, praying hard for a knock on the door.

The springs shifted over Dave's head. Peeking out of the bedspread, Dave saw Cyd's shoes as she stood up alongside the bed. Then he saw her dress falling around her feet. He went crazy and decided the hell with the plan. He started to move out from under the bed, but he must have moved the wrong way. He felt a sharp pain cut across his lower back and he cried out in pain.

"What was that?" Joe asked, jumping off the bed.

"What was what?" Cyd tried to act dumb.

"That noise . . ." Joe said. "It sounded like it came from under your bed."

"I didn't hear any noise," Cyd lied. She heard another one now . . . and this one was music to her ears. There was a nice steady rap on the door.

"Who's at your door?" Joe asked, his eyes wide.

"Why don't we just see . . ." Cyd had a Cheshire-cat smile on her face as she walked to the door and opened it quickly.

Hollis pushed Cyd aside on her way in.

"What are you up to?" Hollis shrieked, looking at her husband.

"I'm not up to anything," Joe yelled back.

"You're not up to anything. . . . I'll just bet you're not up to anything," Hollis screamed.

Cyd inched her way around Hollis and Joe and got close to the bed.

Joe had always been a fast thinker. Now he started thinking real fast. "Look, I met this lady in the elevator. She asked me if I could help her open her door. She was having some trouble with the hotel key. So I helped her out—"

"And then she thanked you by dragging you inside and taking off her dress," Hollis snapped.

Cyd couldn't wait to hear Joe talk himself out of that one. She picked up her dress and put it back on. Any second now Cyd knew Dave would make his appearance.

Joe picked his jacket up off the floor and his tie off the bed. "I'll explain the details to you in our room. Let's go," Joe demanded.

"I'm not taking one step until you talk," Hollis snapped.

"You're taking a step . . . you're taking two steps," Joe said nastily.

What the hell was Dave waiting for? Cyd wondered frantically. In a minute Joe was going to shove Hollis out the door. Joe already had the door open.

Cyd bent down slowly. Keeping her eyes on Hollis and Joe, Cyd lifted the spread and tried to feel around underneath for Dave. She knew he was there. She'd heard him before.

"I'm not leaving here until you confess," Hollis was carrying on as Joe yanked her by the hand.

Cyd started pounding the bed to get Dave's attention.

"I told you we'll talk in private," Joe answered, succeeding in getting Hollis out the door.

Cyd watched Joe slam the door shut. And then, truly puzzled, Cyd lay down flat on the thickly-piled gold-carpeted floor to look under the bed.

CHAPTER NINE

"Dave, they got away. Why didn't you come out?"

"I twisted my back. I can't move," Dave muttered. "Take my feet and see if you can pull me out."

Cyd ran around to the foot of the bed. She bent down and took ahold of Dave's feet and slowly pulled him out. He was mumbling incoherently to himself. As far as Cyd could tell, he was not only angry at himself, he was angry with the world in general.

"I just don't believe my luck. . . . Damnit," Dave continued, articulate now. He was still lying prone on the floor.

Cyd got down on her knees. "If you don't succeed at first, you try, try again. We'll figure something else out," she said soothingly.

He avoided her eyes and looked at the ceiling, his expression bleak. "Maybe I should just give it up and plan on living my life on the run." He yanked off his fake mustache, rubbed his upper lip, which was already irritated, and then he pulled off his wig.

"You have to be optimistic, Dave. . . . We'll think up a new tactic." Cyd hoped her tone conveyed some measure of cheerfulness. She felt so bad for him.

"Yeah . . . right," Dave answered. "If you don't mind, I feel like wallowing in self-pity."

"I'll tell you something, Dave. I hate to admit being stupid, but it's just as well that you didn't slide out from under the bed. What if you'd played out your hand and they didn't confess? They're cool cookies, the two of them. Joe would have most likely gone out screaming for a hotel detective."

"Honey, your plan wasn't stupid. It was a fifty-fifty shot and one I was willing to take. You deserve a round of applause for the way you carried out your end. I was the one who fouled up."

"You didn't foul up. . . . Once we've both had some sleep I just know we'll come up with an even better plan." She pleaded with him with her eyes not to be downhearted.

For her sake Dave decided to at least pretend he was buying her assurance. She deserved that much from him. She'd taken his problem on her shoulders as if it were her own. And he wanted to believe that she wasn't in it just for the money anymore. He gave her the best smile he could manage. "Maybe we will come up with a better plan. Give me your hands. I want to try and get on my feet."

Cyd got up off her knees, placed her feet on either side of Dave, and took ahold of both his hands. Dave made an attempt to lift himself up with her help but he gave up quickly. Cyd could see from his face that he was in pain. "I'm sure the hotel has a doctor. I'll call down and check."

"No doctor . . . it's too dangerous. He might put me in a hospital. What if the FBI has sent pictures of me to all hospitals?"

"But we have to do something. You can't just lie here on the floor and suffer." She looked as agitated as she sounded.

This happened to me once before when I was in high school. The spasm was gone in twenty-four hours. All you can really do for this is rest. I'll live through it without any painkillers. Anyway, if I don't move, it doesn't hurt."

"Aspirin . . . how about aspirin? Will aspirin help any?"

"I'm sure it will." He gave her a reassuring smile.

"I brought a bottle with me. Boy, am I happy now that I always pack one." Cyd hurried over to her suitcase. She flung her clothes out, looking for the bottle. Finding it, she showed it to him as if it were a prize. "I'll get you some water." Cyd grabbed the glass of champagne she'd been drinking earlier. She washed the glass out in the bathroom and brought it back filled with water. And then she helped him raise his head.

"You make one fantastic Florence Nightingale even if you are a bit skinny." He smiled at her after he swallowed two aspirins with the water.

Cyd made a comic face at him and then smiled tenderly. "Flattery is going to get you anything you want."

His gaze searched her face. "I want you . . ." he whispered.

"I want you too . . . but that doesn't mean anything," she added quickly.

Exasperated, Dave rolled his blue eyes. "Okay, I'll bite. . . . Would you care to explain what it does mean?"

Her cheeks flushed to a rosy glow. He looked at her and thought she looked incredibly radiant. "Well, what

157

I mean is . . ." Cyd started. "You do know how to turn me on physically, but to be perfectly honest I'm looking to feel more . . ." She threw out a line and hoped he was going to catch it. All she was asking for was three little words.

"I'm happy to know I've at least made a dent," Dave said, getting angry. He should have gotten used to it by now. She gave with one hand and took away with the other.

Cyd realized instantly that he had misunderstood. But she held her tongue, despite wanting to clear up her point. She felt more. . . . The problem was she felt a whole lot more, but she did have her pride to consider. "Do you want to try and get onto the bed?" She decided to change the subject.

"No . . . I prefer to stay here on the floor," Dave said, still clearly annoyed with her.

"Are we going to go to bed angry?" Cyd asked lightly, trying to change his mood.

"It wouldn't be the first time."

"I'm not sure what you want to fight about, but we could kiss and make up. . . ." Cyd leaned over him and kissed the tip of his nose. Then she softly kissed his lips. Dave wound his fingers in her hair to keep her head in place when she started to move away. He leisurely explored her mouth with his tongue and forgot about everything . . . the mess he was in with the law and even the pain in his back.

"Are you trying to get me all heated up?" Cyd asked teasingly when she pulled away.

"Whatever do you mean?" Dave asked innocently.

"You know perfectly well what I mean."

"What do you think you were doing to me?"

"I only intended to give you a sisterly kiss. You were the one who wanted more."

"I still do. I just can't do very much about it. Could I interest you in giving me a rain check?"

"I think that can be arranged." Cyd didn't see any reason to tell him now that she intended to steer clear of any furthur intimate involvement. She didn't want to kick him when he was down.

"I have a feeling I should have you give it to me in writing . . . especially with your knack of running from hot to cold on me all the time."

"It looks to me like that's a chance you're going to have to take," she said, forcing herself not to ask him any direct questions. But the big question was there in her mind. Was he interested in more than a physical relationship? "Now do you want to see if you can get into the bed?"

"I think I'd better just sleep on the floor." He wondered if she meant the cot, not the bed. The cot had been brought up and was placed in a corner of the room.

"Well, good night." Cyd picked up her pajamas, the ones he'd asked her to pack, and she started for the bathroom to get undressed.

"I brought only this one suit with me. I hate to get it all creased," Dave said, stopping her progress.

"I suppose you'd like me to help you get undressed?" Cyd came back over and gave him a distrustful look.

He gave her back an ingenuous smile. "If you wouldn't mind."

"Are you sure you're incapacitated?" Cyd asked dubiously, bending back down to take off his shoes.

"Can't you see that I am?"

"All I see is that you're flat on your back, which is in itself a very compromising position." Cyd pulled open the knot of his tie and then slipped it off.

"Compromising for you, maybe, but not for me." His tone was husky.

Cyd helped him to free his arms from his suit jacket and then drew it out slowly from beneath him. "All right now?"

"Not quite . . . it's my trousers I'm more concerned about."

"You don't really expect me to fall for this game, do you?"

"You can't blame a guy for trying."

Cyd laughed. "You better thank your lucky stars that you're already in pain." She got up to her feet.

"What are you going to do now?"

"I'm going to get undressed and go to bed." Her heart was beating double time as she unzipped her dress. She already knew she was going to get back down on the floor and make love to him. So much for hanging tough. . . .

"I suppose you know that you're torturing me." He had his eyes fixed on her as she let her dress drop to the floor and stepped out of it.

"Poor baby," she murmured, taking off her half slip, then her bra, and finally her panty hose.

Dave shut his eyes tight when she was completely nude. "I can't take any more of this. . . ."

Cyd went over to the bed and grabbed one of the pillows. She bent down next to Dave and helped him to lift his head so that she could fix the pillow for him.

"You're a witch, Cydney Knight," Dave said, keeping his hands at his side. He knew if he touched her and she pulled away, he'd go crazy because he wouldn't be able to stop her.

"I think the word you really have in mind rhymes with witch." Cyd winked. She got back up to her feet and walked over to the bed.

"You said it . . . not me." Dave couldn't see what she was up to from the direction he was facing.

Cyd picked up the other pillow, pulled down the spread, and yanked the blanket off the bed. She came back over to Dave and plopped the blanket and the other pillow down next to him.

"You . . ." Dave smiled as she went to work un-buckling his belt.

"Yes . . . what did you want to say?" She lowered his zipper.

Dave put his hand over hers. "Wait a minute. . . . Since you're going to be doing most of the work, I still want my rain check."

Cyd laughed. "Do you want to argue about that now or can it wait till later?"

"It can wait." Dave grinned. "Go on with what you were doing."

"I'm not hurting you, am I?" she asked as he lifted his body slightly so that she could remove his trousers.

"I have an enormous tolerance for pain," Dave said huskily. "Hurt me some more. . . ."

Cyd took down his shorts. "You mean like this?" Her hand tightened over him. She wasn't at all surprised to find he was already aroused.

He looked into her eyes as she caressed him, and in that soft cinnamon gaze he was almost certain he saw love. And though he knew the chances were she'd withdraw the gift at any moment, he claimed the wondrous feeling for now.

"Come down here," he murmured, taking hold of her shoulders. He wanted to tell her he'd fallen in love with her. . . . He almost did but he stopped himself in time. . . . He was afraid—afraid to commit himself to a woman again.

She pushed herself up on the palms of her hands. Her legs were opened over his. "I want you to promise me that you're going to lie perfectly still," she whispered.

"Only if you promise to lie still for me and let me make love to you with my rain check. . . ." He teased her with his eyes. Then he gave her a sample of what he had in mind with his fingers at her nipples. "I was going out of my mind when you were with Joe. Don't ever do anything to make me jealous again. I can't handle it."

She wondered if that meant he felt more for her than he'd admitted so far. Or was that just his male ego talking?

"You'll have to give me the same promise, not to make me jealous again," she said, running her hands over his chest.

"I promise." Dave smiled.

"Do you really mean it?" Cyd lowered her face down to his.

Dave locked his fingers behind her head and brought their lips together. "I mean it," he said, breathing raggedly against her mouth. Then he kissed her hard and long.

She reveled in the feel of her naked body against his as she responded without reservation to his kiss.

"You're beautiful. Do you know that?" he asked

hoarsely as his hands moved over her back and then stopped at her buttocks.

"Not too skinny?" she questioned playfully, her hips rotating gently under his hands.

"Did I say you were skinny?" His mouth was next to her ear.

"You did. . . ." She kissed him softly on his shoulder. "How's your back?"

"I'd much rather concentrate on your anatomy."

"Do you mean like this?" She sat up over him and guided him deep inside of her. Her body had been teased long enough by the feel of his hardness between her legs.

"Yes," he moaned. "Just like this. . . ." He gyrated her backside in both his hands and took full command, even though this was to have been her treat.

She wasn't even aware of relinquishing control as she went from one plateau of desire to another even higher one and then higher still, all directed by the rhythm of his hands moving her body up and down.

At some point he let go of her backside to clasp her breasts. It didn't matter to her now, knowing this wasn't going to lead anywhere—that all it was for him was just fantastic sex. She was beyond reason. She was where sensation was the only argument and the only question that needed answering. And he was answering her with his body in a way only he had mastered.

"Honey . . . honey," he whispered, frantically gripping her hips.

She threw her head back, letting him take over, letting him carry her along with him to the same ultimate high only they could reach. And blending there with him on that last glorious peak, Cyd once again experi-

163

enced the same skyrocketing climax that only Dave had taught her she was capable of feeling.

She moaned when it was over and sank down on top of him. He dropped soft sensual kisses along her neck. Then he reached out and found the cover she'd dropped at his side. He worked it over both of them. She started to slide off but he stopped her. "Stay with me like this just for a little bit longer," he whispered.

She wanted to stay with him like this forever. "We both need to get to sleep if we're going to be able to come up with a plan tomorrow," she said, knowing he wouldn't admit it if the pressure of her body was uncomfortable for his back.

"It is tomorrow." There was a hint of sadness in his voice as he let her roll off.

"I still need a couple of hours of sleep to realize that," Cyd murmured, too tired to think about anything right now.

She'd never turned the light off in the room. Dave shifted to his side, wanting to watch her fall asleep. The pain in his lower back told him it wasn't a good idea. He laid his hand across her breasts and felt the pattern of her breathing as he closed his eyes.

When Cyd opened her eyes it was two o'clock in the afternoon. She knew because she looked at the watch on Dave's hand. He was still fast asleep. Careful not to wake him, she slipped out from under the cover.

He was still sleeping when she came out of the bathroom after having taken a shower and dressed. She went over to the phone and ordered a full-course breakfast for both of them. The hotel was accustomed to serving breakfast all the way up until four in the afternoon as an accommodation for their all-night gamblers.

164

"I'm glad you ordered a big breakfast for us," Dave said, having wakened in time to hear her. "If my luck doesn't get better, we may have to switch to bread and water."

Cyd smiled. "How's your back?"

"I'm afraid to find out," Dave answered, still lying prone.

"Would you like me to come over and help you?"

"Will you help me like you did before we went to sleep?"

"No . . ." Cyd grinned.

"If you've switched bases on me again, just don't tell me," Dave groaned.

Cyd walked up to him and took ahold of both his hands. "In case you've forgotten, we have to put our heads together and come up with another plan." She helped him to a sitting position. "Now, how's your back?"

"Better than it was but not terrific." He supported himself with his palms pressed down over the blanket. "Can you find me my shorts? They have to be under here somewhere."

Cyd got down on her knees to look. "Do you want me to help you put them on?" she asked when she had found them.

"If it's not going to tempt you, I'll put them on myself."

Cyd flung them on the blanket within his reach. "Sometimes you really amaze me. . . ." She tried to sound indignant even though she had no real justification. "How do you manage to keep putting aside the trouble you're in?"

"I manage by trying to fake myself out. . . . It's a

talent I grew up developing. Besides that, you make it easy enough for me to find something else to concentrate on." Dave smiled and then lay back to pull up his shorts underneath the blanket.

"I guess that's a major difference between us. I get all caught up in realities," Cyd responded.

There was a knock on the door. Cyd went to answer it.

"Where would you like me to set this up?" The young man from room service wheeled in a cart after Cyd had stepped aside.

"I'll take care of it," Cyd answered, noticing that the guy was eyeing Dave curiously. Dave was still lying on the floor with the blanket pulled up to his shoulders. His wig and fake mustache were lying on the floor right in back of his head. Cyd picked up Dave's jacket from the floor and felt for his wallet. When she found it she took out a dollar and handed it to the guy.

"Thanks," the guy said as Cyd walked him to the door.

"In case you're wondering," she whispered conspiratorially as she opened the door, "my husband is a bit kinky. He likes to put on a disguise and pretend he's my lover."

"Oh . . ." The guy's eyes opened wide. Then, nodding his head up and down, he walked out.

"All along I thought you were the one who was kinky." Dave grinned as Cyd turned to face him after closing the door.

Cyd laughed. "Whatever gave you that idea?" She took his hands and pulled him up. "Do you want to try and go all the way?"

"Is that a direct invitation?"

Cyd laughed again. "We don't seem to be communicating on the same wavelength. Do you want to try getting to your feet?"

"I think I should build up my strength first. Bring the breakfast down here and we'll have a picnic." Dave shimmied back so that he could rest against the foot of the bed.

"All right." Cyd lifted two glasses of juice from the cart. She sat down cross-legged in front of Dave and handed him one.

"Do you want to get under the blanket with me?" Dave gave her a rakish smile.

"No . . . I don't want to get under the blanket. I want you to be serious."

"Okay . . . serious," Dave said, even though he would have liked to avoid it a little longer. "I have a plan. After breakfast we call Hollis's and Joe's room and hope they've slept late. Then I was thinking of going to see them and pretending that I've discovered some evidence to link them to the swindle that they've overlooked. While I'm trying to bluff them I will naturally have my tape recorder on. . . . How does it sound so far?"

Cyd's eyes were bright. "It sounds to me like you could be right on the money." She took his empty juice glass, put it on the cart, and handed him a platter of eggs and bacon. Then she sat down across from him with her own breakfast.

Dave started eating his eggs. "I don't want to bank on it because I hate disappointment."

Cyd nibbled on her bacon. "What if they're not in their room?"

"Then we keep trying all day until they are in their room. I can't come up with anything else, can you?"

"Are you going to be able to get around . . . with your back, I mean?"

"That's the clinker, honey. I'm afraid to get up on my feet and find out."

"Let me go ring their room first before you move. If they're not there, you'll have more time to rest your back." Cyd put down her plate and went over to the phone. She dialed Hollis's and Joe's room and let the phone ring for a long time. There wasn't any answer.

"I just had this really terrible thought," Dave said as Cyd hung up.

"What?" she asked.

"What if they've checked out?"

"Let's not even think about that," Cyd said.

"I think you'd better call down to the lobby and find out."

"I'll go down and check. You finish your breakfast. I'm not hungry. If Hollis and Joe are hanging around the hotel, maybe I'll spot them. I think it's a good idea for us to keep our finger on them at all times." Cyd started for the door.

"If they haven't checked out, call me from the lobby. I'll be sitting with my fingers crossed."

Cyd nodded her head and then walked out.

Hollis and Joe had checked out, but that wasn't even the worst of it. As Cyd turned away from the front desk she spotted a man in a gray flannel suit. She looked away and then threw a glance over her shoulder. The man in the gray flannel suit was dashing across the lobby, but before he darted into one of the many gift shops, he looked back at Cyd. So Dave hadn't been paranoid yesterday, Cyd realized, feeling panicky. She walked quickly across the lobby to the elevators. Someone was watching them. . . .

Dave had managed to get himself dressed by the time Cyd walked back into the room. He was sitting on the edge of the bed. The pain in his back was a whole lot better, but it was far from gone.

"What did you find out?" he asked.

Cyd wondered how he missed hearing her heart pounding. "They've checked out and we've got to get out of here mucho pronto." She went over to her suitcase and began throwing her clothes back inside.

"What do you mean?" Dave stood up carefully.

"Don't panic." Cyd snapped her suitcase. "You know yesterday when you thought there was a man following us . . . well, there is a guy following us. I saw him down in the lobby. He ducked into a gift shop when he realized I'd spotted him looking at me."

Dave sat down heavily on the bed. "Terrific! How are we going to get out of here without being tailed?"

Cyd sat down next to him. "I didn't think about that. . . ."

Dave reached out and picked up the phone.

"What are you going to do?" Cyd asked.

"Get someone to bring up our bill and . . ." Dave didn't finish answering Cyd. He spoke instead into the phone and asked to have their bill brought up to their room. "I realize it's a bit irregular," he was saying on the line. "But unless you want us to leave without paying, you'd better send someone upstairs."

"Are they going to send someone up?" Cyd asked when he hung up.

Dave nodded.

"Then what?" Cyd asked.

"Then we cross our fingers that whoever brings up our bill will tell us if there's a way to get out of the hotel without walking through the lobby."

"Are you able to walk?" Cyd reached for his hand.

"I may have to lean on you a bit." Dave gave her hand a squeeze.

"I just can't understand it. . . . Who would be just following us?" Cyd dropped his hand to rub his back.

"You've got me," Dave sighed.

Cyd turned her head to give Dave a kiss on the cheek. A rap on the door interrupted her. Cyd got up and went to open the door.

"Did you call down for your bill?" the bellboy asked.

"Yes," Cyd replied, letting him in.

"I'll take it," Dave said from the bed. He took out his wallet after the bellboy gave him the bill, then forced a laugh. "This is turning out not to be our day. . . . My ex-wife is downstairs threatening to make a scene. . . . She just can't get it through her head that we're no longer married. I don't suppose the management is going to appreciate that kind of a disturbance. . . ."

"Not at all," the bellboy answered, accepting the money Dave handed him.

"Keep the change for tips," Dave said.

The bellboy nodded and wrote Dave out a receipt.

"Hey, listen. . . . Is there any way we can get out of the hotel without going into the lobby?" Dave asked.

"Not really," the bellboy responded. "Except . . ."

"Except what?" Cyd prompted.

"Well, there's a service elevator that goes down to the garage, but the management doesn't allow patrons to use it."

170

"I think in this case they'd be thrilled to death that we avoided the lobby," Dave said. "Where do we find the service elevator?"

"I could get my head handed to me on a stick—"

"No one is going to know who told us," Cyd insisted.

"All right . . . There's a door at the end of the hall marked 'Employee's Stairway.' The service elevator is inside the landing. If the guys in the garage ask, just tell them you found it by accident and didn't know you couldn't use it. You'd better show them this receipt that you've paid for your stay. They're liable to think you're trying to sneak out without paying."

"Will do," Cyd said as the bellboy walked to the door and opened it to leave.

"Thanks," Dave called out.

"Is everything in your suitcase?" Cyd asked after the bellboy closed the door behind him.

"Yes." Dave got up from the bed. "Go out in the hall, take a walk around, and make sure the coast is clear."

Cyd did as Dave asked. She came back into the room a few minutes later. "There isn't anyone around. The service elevator is just where the bellboy said. I think I should take both our suitcases over to the elevator first and then come back and help you get down the hall."

"I can make it. If the coast is clear, we'll go now." Dave started to lift up their suitcases and then could barely straighten up. He cursed under his breath. He hated feeling helpless.

"Go and sit on the bed," Cyd commanded. "I'm going to take the suitcases first."

Dave smiled at her. "Are you trying to pick a fight with me?"

"Not right now. We can fight while I drive us back to

Brooklyn." Cyd grinned and picked up both their suitcases.

"Good idea . . . Then we'll be ready to kiss and make up by the time we get back to your apartment."

"Don't count your chickens before they hatch," Cyd sallied, putting down one suitcase to open the door. She looked up and down the hall before she stepped out. "Be right back," she said, leaving with their suitcases.

The man in the gray flannel suit watched Cyd's progress down the hall from behind one of the hotel-room doors that was opened only a crack. Then Bill Riker watched her come back and get the guy. Bill had a disgusted look on his face as he noticed how heavily the guy was leaning on her. Well, Bill concluded, Harry Knight had every reason to be concerned about his daughter. The guy was a phony through and through—phony name, phony mustache, and phony wig. On top of that, Bill could see by the way he was leaning on Cydney Knight that he was drunk as a skunk and it was only three o'clock in the afternoon.

CHAPTER TEN

"All these years you've been my top insurance investigator. Is that the best you could come up with?" Harry Knight banged his fist down on the top of the oak desk Cyd had made him for his last birthday.

"I'm trying to get a lead on the guy. I checked out the name James Portland and the name Donald Benson that he used when he registered at the hotel. They're both phony," Bill Riker responded in low, modulated tones, hoping he could get his boss to calm down.

"Did they drive directly back to Flatbush?"

"They stopped for gas. That was it. As far as I could tell he's staying with her at her apartment. Look, Harry, the guy may just be a creep and nothing more. I gave the glasses I swiped from their room at the Golden Nugget to Mitch Conti down at the precinct. He wasn't sure if he could get a clean set of prints but he was going to give it his best. Maybe what you should do is have a little heart-to-heart with that daughter of yours."

"Only as a last resort . . . she gets all uppity when she thinks I'm trying to interfere in her business. I'll tell you what I'm thinking. . . . I'll put odds on the fact that the guy's a bigamist. Go down to the precinct and

173

ask Mitch to check if there are any bigamists running around."

"Why would a bigamist want to latch onto your daughter? They go after bucks, not looks."

"Maybe he wants a change. . . . How should I know?" Harry asked, rankled.

"I'll say this once again. . . . If it were my daughter, I would go and pay her a call in her apartment. You don't have to come on strong . . . just nose around," Bill advised.

"Maybe you're right. . . . Yeah, maybe that's what I'll do."

"Do you want me to go back and watch her apartment?"

"No . . . you stay here in the office and get back to your own work. I'm going to take a ride over there as soon as I call Al Joblon and arrange another appointment on the Lanslow estate."

"Those IRS boys sure move their tails fast," Bill said, picking up his briefcase from Harry's desk.

"You can't live with them and they don't let you live without them." Harry broke his first smile of the morning. "At least Al is one of the easier ones to deal with and we go back a long way."

"Good luck with your daughter," Bill said, opening Harry's office door.

"I'm sure I'll need plenty of luck. Once she gets her mind made up about something, it's hard to reason with her."

"Are you sure your back is better?" Cyd asked, sitting on the floor across from Dave.

"I'm sure." Dave rotated his shoulders as further proof.

"I'm going to try Hollis's mother again. Maybe she's up by now." Cyd stood and went over to the phone.

"Chances are she sleeps all day when Hollis's father is out of town on business. Anyway, why bother?" Dave grumbled. "The whole thing is pointless. Even if we find out where Hollis and Joe are, we haven't come up with a plan. I think it's a better idea for you to dye my hair and make my disguise more permanent. Then I'll see if I can find a place to get a phony ID."

"I'm not going to listen to you talk that way." Cyd came back and sat down on the floor. She reached across the coffee table for his hand.

Dave entwined his fingers with hers. "Can I stay with you until I get a new identity?" he asked quietly and wondered, all over again, if he meant more to her than the double reward money he'd promised.

Cyd looked at him with a soft smile. . . . Sympathy, Dave thought.

"I'm not going to let you give up, because I'm not going to give up," she told him firmly. Being firm was as much for his sake as it was for hers. Cyd wasn't deluding herself. It would have been very easy to agree to let him stay and help him build a new life, with her at the center. Only, deep down, she was sure he'd never forgive himself for giving up.

Dave pulled his hand away. "I suppose you don't want to lose out on the money I promised you," he said, annoyed.

Though it was costing her, Cyd struggled to be unselfish. "Yes, it's the money," she answered, deciding to play on his anger to push him into taking some action.

"Go try them again." He gave her a chilly look.

"Dave . . ." She couldn't stand him hating her.

"Yes?" he asked cuttingly, slicing across the broken quality of her voice.

"Nothing . . ." What was there to say? That she loved him? . . . There hadn't been any indication, at any point, even when they'd been intimate, that he was asking that of her or offering to love her in return.

With his expression controlled, Dave watched Cyd walk across the room to the phone and wondered where his head was at. What had he expected? Leopards don't change their spots. . . . She'd made her position perfectly clear from the start. . . . She was in this for the money—and for kicks. What he needed was a kick in the head for thinking that he'd started to mean more. . . . Her voice penetrated his mental admonishment and he broke off his private tirade to listen to her speak on the phone.

"I called the Golden Nugget and I was told they'd checked out," Cyd was saying. She was speaking to Hollis's mother.

Dave got up and came over to the phone.

"Then they're staying with you. . . . Oh, I'm sure you are happy to have them," Cyd continued.

"For how long?" Dave asked, standing at Cyd's side.

Cyd put her finger to her lips to tell Dave to be quiet as she listened to Hollis's mother. A minute later Cyd said, "They're with a real estate broker right now looking for a home on Sheepshead Bay. How nice . . ." Cyd recounted for Dave's benefit. "And you don't expect to see them until this evening? . . . Oh, no . . . I'm going out myself. I'll try to reach Hollis again tomorrow. And please don't tell her I called. I'd like it to

176

be a surprise." Cyd hung up the phone just as Mrs. Logan was asking her to repeat her name. She wasn't sure if she had gotten it. Cyd knew Mrs. Logan hadn't gotten it because she had never given it.

"So . . . the marriage is still holding out," Dave said thoughtfully. "After what happened in Atlantic City I thought they might have split up."

"I guess I'm not much of a femme fatale after all." Cyd could hear the tenseness in her tone. Only she wasn't thinking about Joe. Cyd was thinking about Dave.

"Mrs. Logan is bound to tell Hollis that an old college chum has been trying to reach her," Dave commented, still deep in his own thoughts. "Hollis may not think much about it, but you never know. I think we should act fast."

"Do you have an idea?" Cyd asked tightly, deciding to concentrate only on the problem of proving Dave's innocence.

Dave noticed her attitude. "Would you care to clue me in? What's eating you?"

"Nothing is eating me," Cyd responded sharply.

"Do you want out? Are you getting tired of playing along?"

"I told you nothing is bothering me. Now do you or don't you have a plan?"

He backed her up against the wall. His proximity was enough to make her heart beat faster.

"I've got it. . . . You're starting to think that the financial inducement isn't worth your effort any longer," Dave said, lashing out.

Amazed at her willpower, Cyd found she had the composure to stare at him coolly. "Were you planning to throw something more into the pot? Or is that what you've been doing already by making love to me?"

Dave looked at her, startled, and then he felt himself getting even angrier as her accusation sank in. That was the way she might have played the game, not him. "You didn't do too much complaining . . . so my guess is it worked." He wondered how she'd handle a little of her own medicine. It didn't take him long to find out. Her open hand slammed across his face.

"You can think whatever you like," she said nastily as he rubbed his cheek.

"I prefer taking action. . . ."

She struggled against him as he tried to kiss her.

"No . . . no . . ." she uttered before he swallowed her refusal. Tears formed at the sides of her closed eyes as she came to terms with the quick demand of her own response. And nothing but that mattered for the moment. . . . Clinging to him now, she took what he had to give and gave back with her heart.

"You've got me so that I can't even think straight," Dave groaned, kissing the pulse beating at her neck.

Cyd held back her tears. "I . . ."

He cut her off with his mouth. "I can't stop wanting you, no matter how much I try," he said in a strangled voice when he lifted his head.

Harry Knight stood outside his daughter's apartment door taking some deep breaths in an attempt to compose himself before ringing the bell. He was clenching the handle of an umbrella so tightly his knuckles were turning white. Harry looked down at his hand as he loosened his grip. Out of habit he'd grabbed his umbrella before leaving his office. The weatherman on the

178

radio this morning had predicted rain. Harry always complied strictly to the weather reports.

Fitting his ear to the door, Harry tried listening for any sound from inside Cyd's apartment. He couldn't hear anything. That didn't sit any better with Harry than if he had detected some noise. Harry dug his hand in his suit pocket and pulled out his keys. Cydney had once given him the key to her apartment in case of an emergency. Well, this was an emergency, Harry decided, sliding the key into the lock. For all he knew, that James Portland guy could be a murderer as well as a bigamist.

"You two-bit hustler . . . get your hands off my daughter," Harry screeched, jumping into Cyd's apartment. Harry lifted his umbrella high in the air, ready to slam it over Dave's head, but his finger hit the release button and the folds of the umbrella unfurled.

"Daddy . . ." Cyd broke away from Dave's embrace and looked at her father in shock.

Dave was just as much in shock and stood stock-still —that is until Harry, out of control, began poking the opened umbrella at him.

"What are you doing, Daddy?" Cyd screamed, chasing around the room after her father and Dave, who was trying to stay out of the way of the umbrella.

"Bigamist . . ." Harry yelled at Dave, ignoring his daughter.

"What are you talking about?" Cyd demanded in a raised voice, fighting with her father for control of the umbrella.

Dave missed a move and the tip of the umbrella

caught him in his gut. He clenched his hands over his stomach as he nearly doubled over.

Harry looked surprised that he had hit his target and he paused, giving Cyd the opportunity to grab the umbrella from him.

Cyd flung the umbrella across the room. "Dave, are you okay?" she asked, gripping Dave's arm.

"I'm fine," Dave answered. "I just got the wind knocked out of me for a minute."

"So it is Dave . . . not James Portland or Donald Benson," Harry ranted. "What's your real last name, Dave?"

"How did you know about the name Donald Benson?" Dave asked, but he was already a jump ahead of himself.

"Wait a minute," Cyd chimed in, looking at Dave. "Donald Benson was the name you used in Atlantic City, wasn't it?" Cyd turned from Dave to face her father. "It was you . . . you had the two of us tailed."

"That's right," Harry admitted shrilly. "Did you think that I'd sit by idly while you—you traipse off with a guy who wears a wig and fake mustache and uses phony names?"

"We knew we were being followed," Cyd said. "I just never thought you were behind it. Who did you send?"

"I sent someone from the office. . . . What does it matter? Right now I want to know what is going on," Harry demanded.

"Okay, enough," Dave said, stepping between Cyd and her father. "I think your father has a right to know what's going on. Go get dressed while I explain it all to him." Dave was already dressed in a gray polo shirt and jeans.

180

"I want to speak to you alone first," Cyd said to Dave, taking his hand to lead him to the bedroom.

"Don't you go cooking anything up with him," Harry warned. "I intend to get at the truth."

"All right, Daddy . . . I promise. Now why don't you pour yourself a cup of coffee? Dave will be right back and then he'll tell you everything." Cyd opened her bedroom door and pushed Dave in. "What are you going to tell my father?" she asked in a whisper as she closed her bedroom door.

Dave kissed her softly on the lips. "I'm going to tell your father the truth . . . everything. I've had more than enough of lying."

Cyd wanted to ask Dave if he'd been lying just before when he'd said he couldn't stop wanting her. Instead, she said, "Good luck," as Dave opened the bedroom door.

"I have a feeling my luck might be starting to run out," Dave said over his shoulder to Cyd as he walked toward Harry, who was holding a cup of coffee.

"This, kiddies, might just be your lucky day." The real estate broker grinned at both Hollis and Joe. "If we play our cards just right, we might be able to talk the owner down a grand or two."

"Is it all right if we stay here and look over the house a little longer?" Hollis asked charmingly.

"Sure," the broker answered. "Just drop the key off at my office when you've finished."

Joe, who hadn't had much to say all morning, had a lot to say after the broker let himself out. "This house is way over our heads, and so were the other two you looked at this morning," he exploded. "I told you I don't want to have to go back to work. How long do you think the money is going to last if you drop a bundle on a house like this?"

"You'd think with the money we had stashed away, you'd find something else to quibble about. . . . If you want to fight, we could talk about that redhead who caught your eye in Atlantic City," Hollis responded haughtily.

"She had one up on you. . . . She was willing to give without putting a price tag on it."

"Look, lover, anytime you want out all you have to do is say the word." Hollis gave Joe an aloof smile.

He looked back at her contemptuously. "You'd like that, wouldn't you? Well, so would I. What do you say we split the money in half and settle out of court?"

"I don't see that as being equitable. But I could see myself parting with a quarter of the money to untie the knot." Hollis fingered the rich teakwood of the cabinets. This was the kind of kitchen she was meant to have— not that she intended to spend much of her time in this room. Her parents had brought her up to tell someone else how many minutes to cook her eggs and not to watch the sand shift in a timer as she did when she was married to Dave.

"Where do you come off thinking you should get more than half?" Joe asked, following her as she walked into the empty area that served as a dining room.

Yes, Hollis thought. She could see herself very nicely playing the role of the gay divorcée in a house like this one. "I did the planning. You only helped carry it out. I think I'm being more than generous. I don't see that I really have to offer you anything if you want out."

"As I see it, my sweet, the bank accounts are in both our names," Joe reminded her.

The reminder was sufficient to have Hollis groan inwardly. She realized he could do her in just by beating her to the banks. Hollis took a deep breath to appease her anxiety. The three gold bangle bracelets she wore around her wrist clanged together as she lifted her hand to Joe's shoulder.

"We've been swiping at each other and I really hate it. I do love you, Joe. And you have to admit that we are terrific together." Her gaze turned soft and she smiled, showing off her perfect white teeth.

Joe was a sucker and he knew it. He was a sucker for her. He still wanted her as much now as he had the first day he'd met her in Dave's office over a year ago. He unhooked the straight gold clip that held her platinum hair to one side and let the silky soft strands of her hair run through his fingers.

"Even if we don't buy this place, I don't see any reason why we can't use it for the afternoon, do you?" His voice was husky.

"I always did want to be made love to on the floor," Hollis responded in a whisper as she lowered the zipper down the front of her pink linen sheath dress.

Cyd finished buttoning her denim blue cotton shirt and tucked the bottom into her Levi's.

"It still seems incredible," Harry was saying when Cyd stepped out of her bedroom.

"But true, Daddy," Cyd insisted, coming up to both men in the kitchen.

"How do you know it's true?" Harry asked, giving his daughter a smile.

"I just know. . . . Call it women's intuition if you like." Cyd winked.

"Dave told me what the two of you were up to in Atlantic City." Harry tried to look aggravated. Then he gave up and grinned.

Dave went over to the stove and poured Cyd a cup of coffee. "If Dave hadn't hurt his back, it might have worked." Cyd accepted the cup of coffee from Dave.

"You see, Mr. Knight . . . I mean, Harry . . . I didn't tell your daughter, but the reason I threw my back out was because I was so blind with jealousy I couldn't get out from under the bed fast enough." Dave smiled as he watched Cyd's big brown eyes get even bigger.

Cyd clumsily put the cup she was holding down on the counter. The coffee sloshed over the sides. "Were you really that jealous? I thought you were just teasing me."

"I was really that jealous. . . . Do you want to fight about it?" Dave turned from Cyd to look at Harry. "I hate to say this, but your daughter can be quite difficult."

Harry laughed. "Tell me something I don't know."

"I'll tell you something I know," Cyd said and laughed. "The two of you can be just as annoying at times."

Harry stood up and slapped Dave on the back. "I always say a woman needs a man just like her father."

Dave's expression turned serious. "One thing no woman needs is a man who is being chased by the law."

Harry turned just as serious. "The tape recorder wouldn't have done you much good. Even if you had been able to record their confessions, it wouldn't have been admissible evidence in court."

"I know," Dave said. "I was hoping that if I did get their confessions on tape and took it to the FBI, it would have at least opened their eyes."

"Yes." Harry nodded his head. "I see what you mean. Look, why don't the two of you come over to my place tonight and we'll put our heads together. I have to get back to the office. I have an appointment that I have to keep. You remember Al Joblon, don't you, Cydney?"

"Sure . . . you play poker together every so often. Isn't he with the IRS?"

"That's Al," Harry confirmed, starting for the front door.

"Wait a minute," Cyd called out, stopping Harry. "Just wait a minute . . . I have an idea. . . . Can Dave and I go back with you to your office? I want to talk to Al."

"What do you have in mind?" Harry asked.

"I'm still working it out in my head," Cyd answered, taking Dave's hand. "I'll tell you both what I'm thinking when we get to your office."

"Please, Joe, I want this house," Hollis said as Joe stroked her beautiful nude body. They'd just finished making love and they were still lying on the floor.

Joe smiled at her. "I suppose I'm too young to retire anyway."

"Do you ever wonder what's become of Dave?" Hollis asked.

"Not really." Joe stopped touching her. His body tensed. "Somehow I don't think I care for your mentioning his name right after we've made love."

185

Hollis rolled onto her stomach to look into Joe's eyes. "On the way back from Atlantic City you were the one who suggested we have a modern marriage. You said it would be all right with you if I took a lover from time to time as long as I told you about it."

"I think it's a bit tacky to think of taking an ex-husband for a lover," Joe said bitingly.

"Well, I wouldn't worry about that happening. I don't plan on keeping him company in a locked cell. If he ever surfaces, that is."

"I really admire your perseverance in trying to keep this guy out of jail." Al Joblon smiled at Cyd.

"What about that brilliant idea she's come up with?" Dave asked. He was also beaming at Cyd.

"I think she's got something there," Al replied. "If Joe Thomas put that kind of money in a bank, the IRS has every right to ask some questions . . . especially if his tax returns don't allow for that windfall."

"How soon can you get on it?" Dave asked, trying to keep a tight rein on his excitement just in case it didn't pan out.

"I'll get on it right now." Al smiled. "Is it okay if I use your phone?"

Harry's head bobbed up and down. "If this works out, I'm going to make sure you win the next time we play poker."

"Put that in writing." Al grinned, picking up the receiver.

"Some woman who says she knew you in college has been trying to reach you. I forgot to tell you that she called when the two of you were in Atlantic City. She called again this morning," Mrs. Logan said when Hollis and Joe returned.

"I can't imagine who it could be," Hollis commented. She hadn't made many women friends in college. She'd reserved her attention for the men. For a split second Hollis pictured Dave back then. . . . It was a shame, she thought, that she couldn't have had her cake and been able to eat it also.

"Well, never mind about that," Hollis's mother said. "Did you find a house?"

"Hollis found a house." Joe shrugged apathetically.

"Let's have tea in the garden," Mrs. Logan suggested. "You can tell me all about it."

"I'm sure you won't miss my input," Joe whispered to his wife. "If you'll both excuse me . . . I'm going to spend the afternoon in the pool."

It took all afternoon for Al Joblon to trace the money.

"Those two are real shrewdies," Al said, hanging up the phone for the tenth time. "They split the money into a number of banks all over Sheepshead Bay and that's why no one reported a new large account."

"Do you mean that if someone makes a very large deposit, the bank is supposed to notify your office?" Cyd asked.

"That's right," Al answered.

"What about Joe's tax returns?" Dave questioned. "Has someone looked them over?"

"All taken care of." Al smiled. "By now someone from the IRS along with someone from the FBI should be paying a call on the two of them. You can go back to your apartment. I'll call you there after we wrap things up," Al said to Cyd.

"Are you sure it's going to be that easy?" Dave asked, standing up with Cyd.

"Young folks don't know when they're listening to the voice of experience." Al winked at Harry.

"And besides that"—Harry grinned—"this guy is determined to rake me over the coals the next time we play poker."

"Mrs. Logan, there are two gentlemen here who would like to speak to your daughter and her husband," the maid announced to her employer, even though both Hollis and Joe were also seated at the dinner table.

Hollis looked at Joe. Joe looked at Hollis. Neither one of them spoke as they both stood up and followed the maid to the front door.

"Mr. and Mrs. Thomas?" FBI Agent Scott Turner inquired as he and John Murphy from the Internal Revenue Service stepped into the foyer.

"Yes . . ." Both Hollis and Joe answered in unison.

"We'd like to speak to you both about all the bank accounts you've opened since you got here." John Murphy took over.

"Is there a problem?" Joe asked, feeling his heart drop to his stomach.

"I'd say there is," Scott Turner answered, flashing his identification. "I think we should all take a ride into the city and discuss it at the bureau."

"Discuss what?" Hollis asked in a cool, bluff tone, but her mind was swinging out of gear. The jig was up. . . .

"We'd both like to discuss a matter of a real estate

swindle," Scott Turner replied, just as cool. The only difference was that he wasn't bluffing.

"Not only did they both confess," Cyd said, hanging up the phone in her apartment. "They are both trying to throw the blame for the scheme on each other."

Dave jumped up in the air and whooped with joy. "It's over. . . . I can't believe it. I can really go back to California and open my office again."

"I guess this is it then," Cyd said softly. This was really it, she thought, the last chapter. . . . Only there wasn't going to be a happy ending. "Hey, don't forget to mail me my check," she added, looking for something to say to cover her hurt. She studied Dave, trying to memorize his features.

Dave stood very still, looking back at her. He hadn't thought about it ever being over—about the two of them going their separate ways. "How can you be sure I'll send you the money?" he asked, wanting to reach out for her but afraid he'd be rejected.

"Listen, it's cool. . . . Either you do or you don't. . . ." She was starting to get too emotional even to speak.

"You could come out to California with me and make sure you collect," Dave suggested, his eyes tight on her.

Cyd flashed him a questioning look, asking herself if he meant more than he was saying. . . . No, she decided, forcing herself not to read what she wanted to read into his suggestion.

"I'll even throw in the cost of your airfare." He thought that if she said no he'd just kidnap her and then fight with her about it later.

"Actually," Cyd began, after clearing her throat,

"I've heard that there are some great woods to work with in California." Did he mean what she thought he'd meant?

"That's absolutely true," Dave agreed. "Does that mean you'll come?" he asked and then held his breath.

Ecstatic little butterflies started to do a dance in her tummy. "Well, I guess so. . . . I've also heard that the sunny climate is good for the temperament. Who knows . . . I may learn to be quite docile."

"God, I hope not." Dave grinned and then slipped his arm around her waist, drawing her willingly into his embrace. "I've just gotten the hang of dealing with you."

"Oh yeah?" Cyd laughed, throwing her head back to look into his fabulous blue eyes.

"Yeah." Dave winked.

"Well, don't count your blessings yet. . . . I'm just getting warmed up," she teased.

"So am I, Cyd . . . so am I," Dave whispered huskily.

190

Now you can reserve September's
Candlelights
<u>before</u> they're published!

♥ You'll have copies set aside for *you*
the instant they come off press.

♥ You'll save yourself precious shopping
time by arranging for *home delivery.*

♥ You'll feel proud and efficient about
organizing a system that *guarantees* delivery.

♥ You'll avoid the disappointment of not
finding *every* title you want and need.

ECSTASY SUPREMES $2.75 each
☐ **137 THE FIRE IN HER EYES**, Sabrina Ryan 12564-2-20
☐ **138 SPLENDOR AT DAWN**, Linda
Randall Wisdom 17785-5-14
☐ **139 FOOTPRINTS IN THE SAND**, Erin Dana 12462-X-23
☐ **140 RECKLESS ABANDON**, Megan Lane 17496-1-97

ECSTASY ROMANCES $2.25 each
☐ **456 TRAPPED BY DESIRE**, Barbara Andrews 19056-8-12
☐ **457 RUFFLED FEATHERS**, Cory Kenyon 17436-8-17
☐ **458 SHE WANTED RED VELVET**, Dorothy Phillips 18213-1-14
☐ **459 THE CAPTAIN'S WOMAN**, Melanie Catley . . . 11007-6-27
☐ **460 SEDUCTIVE DECEIVER**, Kathy Orr 17617-4-18
☐ **461 BEST BET OF HIS LIFE**, Molly Katz 10737-7-18

☐ **3 *THE PASSIONATE TOUCH*,** Bonnie Drake 16776-0-25
☐ **4 *ONLY THE PRESENT*,** Noelle Berry McCue 16597-0-22

At your local bookstore or use this handy coupon for ordering:

DELL READERS SERVICE—DEPT. B1187A
P.O. BOX 1000, PINE BROOK, N.J. 07058

Please send me the above title(s). I am enclosing $_____ (please add 75¢ per copy to cover
postage and handling). Send check or money order—no cash or CODs. Please allow 3-4 weeks for shipment.
CANADIAN ORDERS: please submit in U.S. dollars.

Ms./Mrs./Mr._____

Address_____

City/State_____ Zip _____